Praise for "The Song of Dreams and Shadows"

What happens when a character is just so good that a whole new story materializes around them? Catherine Kane's Song of Dreams and Shadows is the latest example of this.

What happens when two people souls touch and won't let go even across the barriers between this world and another? Again, Song of Dreams and Shadows!

Morgan continues to learn more about the world that is more than this one, Faery and the lands between, and to learn more about the abilities that she is going to need, if she plans to keep crossing between them!

This book contains a rousing adventure in the tradition of the old ballads, and not a small dose of useful information for readers who, like fictional Morgan, are expanding their view of the non-fictional, and very much multifaceted world.

Tchipakkan, metaphysical speaker, artist and podcaster

"The Song of Dreams and Shadows" is a delightful take on the tale of a mortal man trapped by a band of trooping fae. Well written, with a sneaky twist at the ending. You will enjoy this book!

J. T. Sibley, author of "The Way of the Wise", "The Hammer of the Smith", "Norse Mythology... According to Uncle Einar", and "A Different Dragon".

And before this
"The Lands That Lie Between"

The day that Morgan lost her job, she knew that change was coming. She broke her lease, threw everything that she valued in life, including her cat Sam, into her van, kissed her adoptive family goodbye, and started a cross-country trek.

She knew that change was coming. She expected that. What she wasn't expecting was elves, or magick walking in the world around her, or the beauty and danger of the Lands That Lie Between".

And "The Swans of War'

In the Swans of War, the reader once again finds Morgan (and her cat Sam) dealing with the dangers of navigating the Lands that Lie Between (just a side step into a world of overt magic). Things are even worse when the world of Fairy and our world get a bit too close! This is a fine adventure, without the gritty lets-make-it-nasty-so-it-seems-more-realistic style so much urban fantasy has. This is not to say there is no danger- how else can there be heroes, and neither Seelie nor Unseelie sidhe are ever safe. Morgan and Sam are trying to avert a war, as well as save a princess, and our world.

-Tchipakkan, metaphysical speaker, teacher and artist, Co-founder of Changing Times, Changing Worlds conference

Catherine Kane has done it again with her follow up to The Land that Lies Between. Like the previous book, we find ourselves caught up in the adventures of Morgan and her loyal cat Sam, but this time there isn't just a nefarious Unseelie plot to untangle but a Swan Maiden to save - and her angry mother to appease! Fast paced and fun, this story will carry you along from start to finish and leave you wishing there was more."

-Morgan Daimler, author of the Between the Worlds series

The Song
Of Dreams and Shadows

An Urban Fantasy
With Morgan and Sam

By Catherine Kane

Books by Catherine Kane

The Morgan and Sam urban fantasy series

The Lands That Lie Between

The Swans of War

The Song of Dreams and Shadows

Foresight Publications practical metaphysics

Adventures in Palmistry

The Practical Empath- Surviving and Thriving as a Psychic Empath

Manifesting Something Better: Easy, Quick and Fun Ways to Manifest the Life of Your Dreams

The Psychic Power of Your Dreams: Practical Skills for Working with Your Dreams for Insight, Information, Creativity and a Better Life

Magick for Pennies: Affordable Metaphysics for Everyone

Living in Interesting Times: Practical Energywork When Times Get Tough

The Song of Dreams and Shadows

An Urban Fantasy
With Morgan and Sam

By Catherine Kane

Foresight Publications
Wallingford, Ct.

The Swans of War © Dec 2021
By Catherine Kane

ISBN: 978-0-9846951-7-1

Foresight Publications
Wallingford, CT.

Table of Contents

Chapter 1
Forgotten

There were times when his dark and cramped prison cell was cold- bone achingly cold, until he could not feel his hands or his feet. There were times when it was damp and clammy, and it was next to impossible to find any comfortable position in it. There were times when it was partially flooded, and he stood in bronze chains in chest deep water for what seemed like an eternity, unable to mark the passing of time in the darkness, and wondering whether the water would continue to rise and take him altogether.

And there were times when his captors came to visit him. And that was far worse than any cold or wet or darkness.

There were times when it was the little hangers on who came by to torment him with words or kicks or savage pinches. Chained thoroughly as he was, there was little that he could do to stop them from their fun, other than make himself as impervious and uninteresting a target as possible.

But there were times when the more important ones came to see him, with malice and fire and ice and knives and questions. And that was far worse than anything else.

And, when they left him once more alone in the darkness, he would have curled up and wept if the chains had let him, and if he even knew how.

He clung to the thought of his people. His people were great of heart. His people were brave. His people did not know fear or despair or the dark night of the soul.

And he was at one with his people.

But, there were times that, alone in the dark with

1

no one to take note of him, he found himself wondering for a moment how much longer he could continue to act as one of that proud tradition.

Those of his people could not be broken…

But he greatly feared in his heart that he would break before much longer. Would collapse in abject fear. Would weep and cower before his captors. Would tell them every little thing they wanted, and would follow any dark direction they gave, no matter how foul the deed, if they would only leave him alone.

He needed out. He needed to escape from here, escape before they could break his spirit totally. But he had tried every single thing he knew, everything that he had been trained to do, and none of it had worked for him.

The chains, and malice, and cold, and darkness, still held him firmly a prisoner of his captors. And, they would not let him go.

And all of the traitor fears gradually surfacing in his mind held him captive as firm as any chain or wall or enemy.

He slumped then in his chains and leaned his back against the damp and rugged stone of the wall that he felt but could not see. Although he feared to do so, he closed his eyes, leaving himself vulnerable to any unholy thing that might come to torment him in the habitual darkness.

His body was a captive still. But not, at least not yet, his mind…

Unseen tears trickled hotly down his face in the darkness as he reached out to his memories of another time, a kinder place. And let his thoughts, at least, fly free.

Chapter 2
Meditation and Your Inner Voice

As the soothing sounds of rushing water, singing bowl and bamboo flute filled the meditation classroom, Morgan sat in a relaxed posture, alternating between concentrating on her breathing and wishing she had hit the bathroom before class began. The music was calm and beautiful, but the sound of the stream was a bit more suggestive than she really needed.

She also wished that she'd gotten some better sleep the previous night. Something had disturbed her, keeping her up and down, pounding the pillow, getting up for a drink of water, then lying back down for another restless round all night long.

"Focus on your breathing." said the calm voice of the instructor "and then bring your focus further inside- inside of your body, inside of the breath, inside in your center in the place where your inner wisdom lives. Bring your attention to that still, quiet place within the music, within the breath, within yourself."

Morgan took another slow, deep breath, and did her best to bring her focus back to that still, quiet space. She'd only been taking practical meditation classes for a couple of weeks, but she was already having flashes of what might be possible for her with time and practice.

If only her body wasn't trying so hard to distract her.

Then, briefly, it was not. And, for just a minute, she could feel that still, quiet place her instructor was talking about.

"And now take another slow, deep breath," said her instructor, as the music played on "and try to reach out to your inner wisdom. Your inner wisdom lives there in your center– in the center of the still, quiet place inside of you. If you have a question that you've been unable to answer, think of it now in a calm, cool manner. And take another slow, deep breath…"

"And listen…"

"And see what you hear…"

Morgan took another slow, deep breath, and held her focus softly within her in that still, quiet place in her center. "A question, eh?" she thought. "Well, what do I need to learn next to prepare for my immediate future?"

And, for just a moment, she thought that she heard an answer…

And then her left calf cramped up, and her bladder protested, and the class was over.

Drat.

But, still, she'd gotten something there for a moment and, if she'd gotten to that point once, she could get there again.

Meanwhile, the ladies' room was waiting.

After reemerging from the porcelain refuge, Morgan headed back into the classroom at the back of the new age shop to collect her meditation equipment before doing some window shopping in the store. Her instructor, a short round woman with long brown hair, glasses, and a wealth of knowledge on all things psychic, metaphysical and alternative health, was still packing up her equipment from the class.

"So, how'd it go, Morgan?" she called cheerfully, as she finished coiling up the extension cord for the sound system. "Did it feel like you were making progress?"

Morgan smiled warmly at the woman.

"Maybe. I think so." she said. "I had a brief flash of something or other just before the meditation ended, but my body began to protest and I couldn't hold onto it long enough to make anything of it."

"Better luck next time then." said her teacher kindly. "That inner voice is deep inside of every one of us, and I know that you have what it takes to get there, but it takes a little time to strike a balance between the needs of the body and the needs of the mind. All it takes is time and practice. Eventually, you won't need me, but it can be a help to have guidance when you first set out."

"I think your style of teaching is helping me a lot with this." said Morgan. "When Sara first told me that I should take up meditation to learn to get in touch with my inner wisdom, I tried it on my own at first and didn't have a lot of success with it. Having you set the tone, and talk me through it is working much better for me. I like that we're learning different types of meditation, too."

The teacher smiled. "Thanks. That's good feedback for me." she said. "I personally like to try different kinds of meditating, and it's good to hear that that's working for my students as well. It helps me to make my classes better. Next week, we'll be trying a walking meditation, and I'll be interested to hear how you like that one."

"Given my recent experiences in the last year and a half, I'm wondering if you have a running meditation on tap." Morgan said. "It'd be useful to be able to calm my mind, support good health, and access my inner wisdom the next time things go wrong and I'm running for my life again."

Her teacher chuckled. She was one of the few people who lived their lives with one foot in both worlds, and she'd been a party to Morgan's two previous adventures into the world of enchantment a second apart from the mundane world.

"I'll have to look into that." she said thoughtfully. "Come to think of it, between those who walk between the worlds and upper-class business professionals, I can think of a number of people who might benefit from a running meditation if I could find or develop one. I might have to run a bigger class at that point."

Morgan grinned. It was a relief to have friends like her teacher who knew about the Lands Between. To know folks familiar with the ways of magick, who knew the difference between the seelie and unseelie courts, and who wouldn't think she was crazy if she mentioned her talking cat.

"See you at next week's class." said her teacher, stuffing her last bits and pieces in an oversized knapsack, and slinging it over one shoulder. "Remember to keep practicing, and you'll improve a lot faster."

"I promise" said Morgan, following her to the door of the empty class room. "I really want to have a handle on this before anything goes wrong again and I really need it."

Her teacher winced and turned to stop her for a moment.

"Now, I don't want to be picky," she said carefully

"but I think we need to talk seriously for a moment."

"One of the basic rules of energy is what you put your attention on, you tend to attract more of. As they say where attention goes, energy flows. Some people call this principle the Law of Attraction. Now that's no reason to ignore trouble, but that's twice in only a couple of minutes that I've heard you focus on more trouble coming. That worries me. Putting more of your focus on problems coming can tip the scales into attracting them."

Morgan froze for a moment and looked at her teacher's face. At first, this sounded like criticism, but, looking into her teacher's eyes, she saw only concern there for her.

"Putting your focus there isn't necessarily the best choice that you could make for yourself." her teacher said. "It's good to prepare for issues, but it's best to mostly put your focus on better things, and call them to you instead."

Morgan relaxed again. She wasn't really sure if she totally bought into what her teacher was saying, but it certainly wouldn't do any harm to try and put her mental focus on something better than her past adventures.

"Well, if you say so." she said cautiously.

Her teacher looked at her closely, and then her concerned face relaxed into smiles. "That I do," she said "and I'm glad that you're willing to give this a try, even if you don't really see the need for it as of this time."

And teacher and student continued out together into the main body of the beautiful new age shop, ready for some major shopping...

Chapter 3
Changing Hands

He had thought that he was dead when he went down under a wave of unseelie opponents.

And then he woke up, battered but alive and captive in unseelie hands.

And, as the days went by, being a swan knight, he took every chance he could to resist and to try to escape from his captors.

Without success.

At last, battered and only semi-conscious, he found himself being bound and transported from the barrow to another place.

"A swan knight..." said an unfamiliar female voice. "How unusual. You do not usually find them on the open market."

A slender hand grasped his chin and lifted it as he hung in the grasp of his captors.

"And he is pretty, too." said the voice. "Or, at least, he was pretty until you beat him within an inch of his life."

"He is trouble." one of his captors said. "You will have trouble holding on to him."

"That does not matter." cooed the new voice. "A pretty pretty is worth a bit of trouble. I shall take this one. Name your price."

He heard coins clinking and then he was borne away in new hands.

Chapter 4
In Morgan's Kitchen

"You know, your teacher, right she is" said Estelle, the younger of the two swan maidens, bending over and staring intently into the depths of the open refrigerator. "On something your attention firmly putting, the best way to draw it to you is. Ooooo! Cake you here have!"

Sam nosed cozily in next to Estelle, his friendly furry face also deeply interested in the contents of the refrigerator.

"Never mind that slice of chocolate cake there." said the talking cat. "Take a gander at that gorgeous bowl of tuna fish salad on the second shelf there. You can just pass that baby right down to me, Estelle!"

"And your teacher is right." he added, standing up on his hind legs and peering deeper into the icy depths. "That's called the Law of Attraction, and it's a very powerful energetic force that can either make your life much better or muck it up good and proper, depending on if you understand it and how to work with it."

Estelle's older sister, Ariella leaned back on the central kitchen island in an excessively casual yet dramatic pose worthy of any super model. As lead swan princess and heir apparent to the leadership of the local flock of the Mantelfiedervolk, the swan people, she took her position very seriously – although she also liked some cake upon occasion ….

"Vell, about you folks I do not know" she said, "but about now, to a nice tuna fish sandvich, my attention I could bring. Could the bread you pass? And some of that cake too, nice that vould be."

Morgan sat at the kitchen table, watching as the two swan maidens and the talking cat laid a serious siege to the contents of her fridge, and chuckling quietly at their chatter. It was always a good time when she had the swan sisters over, even if she did always have to restock the contents of her pantry afterwards.

Although, come to think of it though, given that she lived with Sam and considering his prodigious appetite, she should actually be used to buying truly heroic amounts of groceries by now.

Ariella gathered up the tuna fish, bread, a plate and utensils. She joined Morgan at the table, and began to make herself a sandwich, and Sam followed her to the kitchen table, still watching the bowl of tuna fish expectantly.

"So, all of this Law of Attraction hoo- haw, vat it is?" she asked as she thoroughly buttered the bread. "The simplified version please, yah?"

"I wouldn't mind a more extensive explanation myself." Morgan added. "My teacher mentioned it to me briefly after today's class, but if it's something that's having an effect on my life, I'd really like to know more about it."

Sam leapt up on to the kitchen table, landing gracefully directly in front of Morgan. He sat down before her, effortlessly coiling his tail sinuously about his paws, in a classic cat position old when first the pyramids were built. He adjusted his position slightly, for the maximum effect on his audience, and then began to lecture, using his usual "knowledgeable– older – professor" voice.

"Well, let's start at the beginning" he said, in a slightly affected, put on tone. "Everything is made of energy. Every person, every creature, every living thing and every

12

magickal item is made of energy and that energy reflects who they are and what they can do."

"Some energy is higher and vibrates at a quicker rate. Some energy is lower and slower. Energy levels lie along a range and can vary depending on individual and situation. The level of your energy field is set by things such as your beliefs, what you focus on and how you cope with the world around you." Sam went on.

"And your energy tends to attract things and people and experiences that vibrate at the same level as it does. That's how the Law of Attraction works. Higher energy tends to attract more things you like, want and prefer. Lower energy tends to attract more negative things. All energy tends to attract evidence that supports your beliefs about life."

"So you tend to get more of what you focus on. If you tell yourself "I think I can, I think I can", you're more likely to succeed. If you tell yourself you were born to fail, you probably will. Why? Because no matter what you're telling yourself, you're setting your energy levels to attract just that experience."

The swan girls mock-applauded his performance enthusiastically, and he bobbed his head in an exaggerated acknowledgement of their attention.

"Amongst other things "he said, dropping the accent "that's why women who are pregnant suddenly see pregnant women everywhere they go. And people who buy a particular car find the streets crowded with similar vehicles."

"Now that may seem like pretty small potatoes at first, but it has bigger implications for daily life." Sam continued on. "Did you ever wonder about that saying "The rich get richer, and the poor get poorer."? That doesn't just speak to inequal class structure. To a certain extent, that

13

happens because both rich people and poor people alike are focused most of the time on their current financial states, on what they know and what they expect to happen; and therefore, they tend to attract more of the same. Same old, same old."

"And people with chronic illness sometimes find it difficult to improve their health, because their current pain and health challenges take up a majority of their attention."

"About that, right he is ..." said Estelle through a mouthful of chocolate cake. "A friend who always to him has the vorst things happen, I have got. Law of Attraction – the vorst he expects, and the Universe obliges. Another friend I have got who the best expects. Always right for him everything goes - Law of Attraction hard at vork again there is."

Ariella gestured imperiously at Sam with her sandwich. "Huh. So, are you saying that all of these people vith the problems have no one but themselves to blame?" she asked the cat. "To me, too fair that does not seem to be. Just some bad luck that is not? Just in the wrong place at the wrong time being?"

Sam blinked his big golden eyes, startled at her question.

"Why no, I'm not saying that at all. I'm certainly not saying that their problems are all their own faults." he said. "The fact that each and every sentient being in any of the planes at all has Free Will means that we're always free to choose our own paths, and to change them as we will: and that there is no Deadly Fated Doom ahead of us. I'm just saying that the Law of Attraction is a metaphysical tool, like a hammer, a screwdriver or a pry bar, and that we can use it

14

as it was meant to be used to make our jobs easier, we can ignore it and do things the hard way, or we can actually misuse it, and tip the scales of life towards an extra pound of pain."

"The Law of Attraction can stack the cards of life in our favor, or deal us deuces from the bottom of the deck." he said. "It's just a question of knowing how to play the game well, so that you end up winning as opposed to losing."

"So, how do we play this Law of Attraction game, anyway?" asked Morgan, finding herself getting more interested in the topic by the moment. "How do we get the Law of Attraction working on our side?"

"Well, the first part is "What you focus on, you get more of," said Sam. "not only more of whatever you're directly focusing on, but also more of other things that make you create the same vibration or feel the same way."

A delicious and sizeable clump of tuna fish had dropped out of Ariella's sandwich and landed on her plate. Sam paused, and then struck like lightning, deftly snagging a heaping paw of tuna fish and quickly dabbing it into his eagerly waiting mouth.

"Hey! You! Cat!" Ariella exclaimed "That I vas gonna eat!"

"So, if you're focusing your attention on, say, tuna fish," he went on, deliberately ignoring the somewhat indignant swan princess while he diligently licked the last delicious taste off of his paw, "you may not only attract said tuna fish, but also just possibly some of those delightful little cocktail shrimp that I was talking to you about when you were making out the grocery list."

"Have you ever at one of them parties been vere the

15

shamans all together in one corner get and about spirits and the Vorld Tree talk; and the maidens in another area clump and about clothes and girlie stuff chatter; and the varriors all out on the deck are bragging and wrestling moves each other showing?" said Estelle. "Vell, the Law of Attraction again that is. Like calls to Like, so even if two of the maidens is blond and four is brunetters, they all a similar feel have and they tend together to gather."

"And if you're at that party and looking for a shaman" said Sam "You're going to tend to focus on the qualities of a shaman and end up in the shaman's corner. And if you're asking one shaman some questions and there are others in the area, they're going to drift over and start giving you their own two cents on your question. By focusing on "shaman", you automatically end up with "sha– men"…"

A shaman in training herself, Estelle briefly made a face at Sam.

"Ha ha, such a funny little cat he is." she said, just a little bit sarcastically. "But, if this fuzzy fellow's so-so joke ve is ignoring, for most folks that is pretty much how it out works. If on something real hard you focus, vhether a good something or a bad something, in a major way your chances of drawing it into your life you increase. And other things that make you feel like the first one does you also increase your chances of drawing."

"So your mudder vas right- if the good thoughts all the time you think, to you the nice things are more likely to happen." said Estelle "And if a face like that you make," she said making a grotesquely pouty face "that vay, it is gonna stick …"

She relaxed the pout into her normal gentle face and

16

grinned at them all.

All of a sudden, the pieces of the explanation started to fall together for Morgan. "So, you're saying that positive thinking really does have power to it?" she asked. "It has actual magickal power besides just making you feel good?"

Sam nodded at her absent mindedly. "Feeling good actually has a certain amount of metaphysical power of its own." he said, still eyeing Ariella's plate, just in case another poor little lump of tuna fish wandered off and got lost. "Positive feelings generate positive vibrations, and positive vibrations and beliefs can help with shifting the nature of reality for the better. Positive vibrations can boost your health, improve your luck and generally make things go better. Negative feelings can change reality too, but they tend to shift it into something that nobody wants, so we usually don't think about working in that direction."

"But positive thinking is also helpful in another way. Positive thinking means focusing on what you want, as opposed to what you don't want," the golden cat continued "and the more that you focus on that thing, the more likely you are to either attract or manifest that thing or something like it that makes you feel roughly the same into your life. So, the more that we think positively, the more positive things we focus on, and the more positive things and the less junk we manifest or attract into our lives. Positives things like, maybe, some more tuna fish …"

"Now, a minute here vait." said Ariella, leaning forwards in interest and paying no heed to the way her sandwich was beginning to bulge. "Are you really saying that, if about them enough I just think, in mein closet tomorrow a brand new pair of leather boots vill just show

17

up? The red ones? Vith the spanking six inch heels?

Morgan, Sam and Estelle all froze and stared at the swan maiden for a minute. She was completely right and completely wrong at the same time – which was no small trick.

"Well, partly yes…" the cat finally said slowly and carefully "…and partly no. First of all, that's a pretty short time to make something that specific work. It's been done, but usually by someone who has a bit more experience in the Law of Attraction."

"A bit more experience? In about something just thinking?" said Ariella, sensing she was on to something here and still being hopeful. "But lots of experience in thinking about boots I have. Especially about these boots. About them all of the time I think."

She sat back and looked at the cat expectantly, as if he was about to produce the red leather boots with the six inch heels in question right now by magick.

"Yes… well…" stumbled the cat, somewhat at a loss "It might work. But, then again, it might not. You see the Law of Attraction isn't something that works every time like a vending machine. It doesn't always work on a predictable schedule. What it does do is tip the scales of life in our favor. It doesn't automatically deliver a car, or true love, or new boots in less than twenty-four hours most of the time, but it does dramatically increase the odds that we will get what we want and also get it faster than we had would otherwise get it."

"And likewise, if we tend to focus on what isn't working in our lives, the Law of Attraction is also hard at work, only this time attracting more of the things that distress us and other things like them into our lives. To paraphrase the computing world, garbage out, garbage in. If you keep your eye on what you definitely don't want, you shall surely have it."

"Garbage, schmarbage; maybe yes and maybe no." said Ariella. "You magick types all the time too hard it make. About my red boots I am just gonna think, and then maybe they show up, nein?"

She leaned back, closed her eyes and squinched them up tightly, an expectant expression on her beautiful face.

The other three paused for just a beat, and then Sam got a really funny look on his own face. He started to say something, stopped, thought and then started to speak again.

"You know, she could possibly have something there." he said thoughtfully.

Morgan grinned at him. "So, what you nice folks and my teacher are all saying is that focusing too much on the possibility of danger and adventure coming back into my life is a swell way of ending up running for my life again, right?"

"Well, you don't want to totally ignore possible challenges that are predictable or easily avoided." said Sam. "You want to fill up your gas tank before it reaches empty, and you need to have band aids in the medicine cabinet. But you make reasonable and appropriate preparations for predictable problems that are not unlikely to occur; and then you let it go. As much as possible, you don't worry about it. You don't focus on potential problems any more than the minimum needed to avoid or deal with them. You don't "if–only" yourself into a Law of Attraction crisis by placing your focus most of the time on what is currently negative in your life, or on what negative things might possibly come to you."

His attention wandered off again to Ariella and her sandwich.

"So, the more that I focus on good things, the more likely it is that good things will come into my life," said Morgan "and the more that I focus on bad things, the more likely it is that bad things will come into my life. Is that how it works?"

Estelle looked over at Sam. "Got it, I think that she has." she said, grinning at Morgan.

Far too busy at the moment to comment on this, Sam was very carefully watching Ariella, as she focused on her red boots with face screwed up and eyes shut tight. She clutched her sandwich tightly as she focused on her red boots– perhaps a bit too tightly. The bread tore under the pressure of her concentration and her clenched fingers, and the sandwich began to break apart, and fall in messy but appetizing pieces to the plate below. In the next minute, a tasty ball of tuna fish dropped, and Sam fielded it like the all-star pro he was.

Morgan thought about all of this, and then she frowned a bit. "You said that people can attract bad things by focusing on them, as well as they can attract good things. Does that mean that, if there's something bad in your life, it's there because you've attracted it?"

Estelle took a thoughtful bite of chocolate cake, and then took over the lesson.

"Vell, sometimes yes," she said "but not alvays so. People there are who vill tell you that is so, of course. There are alvays these kinds of people, and the real party poopers they are."

"Some vill tell you that the Law of Attraction alvays one hundred per cent of the time vorks, and that everything in your life there is because your thoughts it so made. Some this believe because it makes them safe or powerful feel to believe that total control over things they have. Some it believe because off the hook them it lets when other people in distress are. They can then believe that only because of negative thinking folks in trouble are, and that, if better thoughts those folks only thought, better for themselves they things could make."

"And who knows? Since your reality your beliefs do shape, if hard enough you believe that everything happens because here you called it, it may indeed so be."

"On the other hand, I believe that more of a moderate thing reality is." said the swan shaman seriously. "I believe that yes, many things, both good and bad, are in your life because vith your thoughts you called them. But I also believe that many other things there are, because your thoughts kind of random vere and kind of random stuff, attracted, vich not alvays the best stuff or the stuff that you want is."

"Or sometimes, bad stuff comes because not focusing on much of nothing you were, and some random stuff came by and into you smacked. Kinda like drive –by karma."

Morgan thought about that for a moment more. Her face grew more somber as she thought.

"I think that I like the way you see it better than the other explanations," she said. "because to think of it the other way would mean that, when horrid things happen to folks, it would always mean that they'd caused them, and that really seems like blaming the victim to me. To believe that everything in your life is there because you have drawn it to you would mean that you had invited in the trauma. "

"For example, it would mean that that poor swan knight, Claud, drew his own Death to him…"

Chapter 5
Morgan Remembers

"For example, it would mean that that poor swan knight, Claud, drew his own Death to him…"

Morgan's mind flew back to when she had first encountered the swan people. It started with a battered swan knight collapsing unconscious on her front porch late one night, with the howls of dark hunds hot in pursuit.

Despite Sam's protests, she'd dragged Claud inside, quickly mopped up his blood and hid him from pursuit. Once the hunds had moved on, she'd patched him up and tended him all night to keep him alive.

In the morning, he woke and told her that the unseelie sidhe had slaughtered all of his fellow knights and kidnapped Ariella, and that he needed to get back to his flock and let them know what had happened.

He had tried to stand and could barely do so. At that point, she refused to let him try to get home alone and said that she and Sam would help him get there.

Because she was the kind of woman she was, she made that stick.

She hadn't known him for long, but she had liked him- liked his sense of honor and sense of humor.

Which made it all the more heartbreaking when they were ambushed and he sent them on to carry his information to his people, while he stayed behind to keep the unseelie off their trail.

She remembered the sounds behind her as Claud went down under a wave of enemies…

Chapter 6
Memory

Trapped in darkness, he remembered his last day in the light. He remembered his fellows being slaughtered and the princess taken, and being left for dead. He remembered awaking to a scene of horror, running for his life and to reach his flock to let them know what had happened. He remembered being pursued.

And he remembered collapsing on an unfamiliar porch because he could run no more.

He didn't remember that a woman who did not know him dragged him inside, concealed his presence from his unseelie pursuers, bandaged his wounds and tended him until he awoke, even though her cat companion warned her of how dangerous he was and how unsafe the whole situation was. He only found that out when he finally came to consciousness.

And he remembered how she had refused to let him go on his way alone, because he was still weak. He had resisted making her responsible for him, but he had still been a bit relieved about that.

He remembered her grey eyes and long hair and the set of her jaw as she told him in no uncertain terms how things were going to be.

And he remembered how the unseelie ambushed them and how he sent her cat and her on to reach his flock, while he stayed behind to slow down the sidhe. He remembered going down under a wave of attackers.

He wondered if she and her cat had escaped the unseelie sidhe and reached his flock.

Chapter 7
Back in Morgan's Kitchen

Ariella's eyes flew open. Sam blinked and turned his back on the tuna to look seriously at Morgan.

"And, somehow I just can't believe that Claud had a need to die to draw his death to him."

"He fought so hard to survive the terrible wounds that he had taken in the initial attack." said Morgan earnestly. "He fought so hard to return to your flock to tell them the truth about who killed the swan guards and kidnapped you, Ariella. When we were outnumbered and trapped by the unseelie sidhe, he fought so hard to defend Sam and I from them and to give us the chance to get away, even at the cost of his own life."

"I just can't believe he would have fought so hard to survive, if he truly was drawing his death to him with his thoughts."

Three pairs of stricken eyes looked into hers. And all four of them paused and remembered the fallen swan knight.

"A VARRIOR he vas!" Ariella roared suddenly, pounding the table before her for emphasis. "A VARRIOR BORN! And, as a varrior, his constant companion death vas, but, for him, never a source of fear this vas. Every svan knight knows that, at any time, death may for him come. Ve are taught that this is so, but not to dwell upon the hour that for another battle in another vorld ve depart. He vould not have let fear and sorrow cloud his thoughts!"

"There you are right." said Estelle. "He vas not by his thoughts destroyed. About life and living, his thoughts always vere. A good man, a strong man, a man vith no taint of darkness in him, he vas; and I never saw any sign that to life he was not fully commited."

"And things like this are why I believe the Law of Attraction can help us to manifest things, but that not everything in our life is there because we have attracted it." said Sam slowly. "I only knew Claud for a short time, but in the limited time that I knew him, I never saw him fearful, or negative, or focused on death, despite all of the dangers of the situation that he found himself in. He seemed to me to be a very strong and positive man, and, if the Law of Attraction were as absolute a force as some people believe it to be, an outlook like his would have attracted far better things than he received."

Morgan suddenly found herself tearing up a bit, and reached in her pocket for a tissue.

"That's a relief to me "she said "because, for just a little bit, it was beginning to sound like his death was his own fault, and I don't know if I would want to live in a world where universal laws work like that."

There was a respectful hush for a moment, as she dabbed at her eyes.

"He gave his life in the service of what he believed in." said Sam, after a moment. "A man could well do worse…"

Chapter 8
Uneasy Sleep

Morgan had always liked having company over to her home, and it had been a merry evening indeed with her two swan friends visiting with her and Sam, but Morgan didn't find the following night nearly as kind.

She'd been having problems sleeping lately. Problems getting deeply to sleep. Problems with waking up in the middle of the night, usually between 3 and 4 a.m. Problems getting herself back to sleep again.

And then, there were the dreams. Or maybe "not dreams" – the "not–really–dreams–per–se". Just vague, half remembered flashes of intrusive sight and sound. Unclear images that might possibly have been dreams (or then again, might not be). Ambiguous impressions of having dreamed about something overnight but no clear memories to hold onto of the actual dreams.

It was maddening. Like waiting on line in a store while someone ahead of you needs a leisurely price check on an obscure sale item. Like waiting impatiently for the totally anticipated punch line of an old joke that has gone on far too long. Like waiting for a sneeze that continually threatened without ever exploding.

And here she was again, sitting up in bed again, eyes wide open in the dead of night and no surcease in sight. The "witching hour", as it is sometimes called, had come around again on little cat's combat boots, and she had found herself lurching bolt upright in bed, launched from slumber straight up to hyper-alert, like some kind of a chunkin' pumpkin launched from a homemade catapult. Zero to sixty with no actual reason she could explain.

And a vague impression of tears. Chains and tears in a dark, cold place.

Morgan reached up in the darkness of her bedroom and felt her face. Nope- no tears there, so she wasn't merely crying in her sleep and half –dreaming about it. But, for a moment, it had felt so real to her.

Morgan sighed in the darkness. By now, she had the waking–up–in–the-middle–of–the-night routine down. When she was as wide awake as she was now, just lying down again in bed and trying to get back to sleep would only make her more wakeful and would not help her to sleep. She needed to get up and do something else until she felt sleepy again.

Morgan carefully reached out and turned on the bedside light. Tempting though it might be to read to herself in a comfortable and warm bed, she'd done some research and found recent studies indicated that getting out of bed could help to break the recurring cycle of late night sleeplessness.

So that meant that she was off to read in the bathroom then.

Taking a good, but not overly stimulating, book from her side table with her, Morgan slid out of the tangled sheets, slipped on her slippers, and headed down the hall.

"So you can't sleep either…" an unexpected voice said beside her.

"Gak!" said Morgan articulately, startled by the voice and almost dropping her book, before she realized that Sam was awake as well. "If I wasn't awake before, I would surely be now!"

The golden feline sat in the middle of the deeply carpeted hall, and carefully washed one paw, looking excessively casual. "You've been up and roaming around at this time every night for at least two weeks now." he said carefully "and every night, it has taken longer and longer for you to get back to sleep. The funny thing is that the same thing's been happening to me."

Her head whipped around and she stared for a beat at her feline roommate. "Oh, I'm sorry." she said. "Have I been waking you up when I get up?"

"Not so much that." said Sam, avoiding eye contact by focusing intently on his paw "The thing is that you're waking me up before you wake up."

"Oh-my-gosh–how–embarrassing-I'm–so–sorry, Sam." Morgan gargled out in one explosive rush of apology. "Have I been making too much noise? I'm so sorry!"

"Well, not loud noises as such, no." said the cat. "It's something different altogether. Morgan, my girl, have you been dreaming a bit more lately? Because I've been picking things up from the ethers that felt like they were coming out of someone else's dreams."

"So have you been Dreaming?" he said.

Morgan stopped and thought.

"I don't think that I have been dreaming." she said. "But I don't usually remember my dreams, so I could be dreaming and not remember it at all. Although, I have been getting little blips and bits of somethings when I sleep lately. Which could be dreams, I suppose. I don't really remember them, but they could be flashes of dreams that I'm not really remembering..."

"Oh, I don't know!" she yowled, the logic train

31

falling off of its tracks from a bad case of circular logic, combined with a severe sleep shortage. "It might be me – and then it might not. And I'm just too tired out to figure this out. And, on top of that, I'm babbling and how embarrassing is that?"

Tears in her eyes from frustration and lack of sleep, she sat down suddenly on the hallway rug, next to the cat.

Sam pivoted smoothly, putting one paw softly upon her knee. He stretched up and looked deeply into her eyes.

"It's ok, Morgan," he said kindly. "and, more to the point, it may be a sign that your own intuition is beginning to surface at last. For many people, their first serious taste of their own inner wisdom comes to them through their dreams, and you've been working really hard to get in touch with that inner wisdom."

"Well, if it's going to wake me up every night, and keep me short of sleep, I don't know if I want it." Morgan pouted.

"Oh no, no" said Sam hastily "once you've got a better handle on it, you'll be able to use your inner wisdom without having to wake up at the crack of shriek every night. We can talk some more about this tomorrow, but for tonight, once you're ready to go back to bed, I'd recommend you try using one of those techniques for accessing inner wisdom that you've been doing in meditation class to get a better handle on the knowledge that your dreams have to bring you, and to sleep better besides."

He rubbed his feline forehead against hers and booped her nose with his in an expression of cat affection.

"You're going to be fine "he said. "It's just a little bit of metaphysical growing pains."

Morgan cautiously smiled and scratched him behind the ear for a moment, obscurely comforted, before standing, picking up her book and going on to the bathroom to read until she was once again drowsy. Behind her, the golden sound of purring filled the dark and silent house.

And a solid fifteen minutes later, Morgan finally closed her book again, turned out the bathroom light, and groggily staggered her way out the door and back down the hall that led back to her bedroom. Sitting and reading for a while in another room had helped to calm her a little bit, find her center again and stop her heart from pounding like an oversized big bass drum, but it hadn't made up for the overall lack of sleep in the recent weeks and, once the adrenalin had worn off, the fatigue would hit like a tsunami of tired.

"You know" she thought "Exhaustion sucks big time. Really, really big time."

Heavily clambering back into her eagerly waiting bed, Morgan gently laid her heavy head back down on her fluffy pillows and then pulled up all the covers until they covered it.

Shut out the world. Yeah. That's the ticket. Just me and my pillow

And the dreams…

Bit by bit. Minute by minute. The world, the room itself around her gradually dropped away from her, and Morgan was caught up and back in dream land once again.

Flashes of color dazzled her. Blasts of raw emotion. Overwhelming sounds, but nothing that she could make any sense at all of. Sensations of dampness and of wet and cold and of close, close confinement. Blue eyes, deep blue eyes, startled and staring briefly into hers before they were whisked away again into the confusion. Mist and fog and darkness, darkness, darkness;

And overall, despair.

But with a small but tough and stubborn core that still refused, no matter how bad things seemed to be, refused to give into that darkness and despair.

She could reach it, briefly, but she couldn't hold onto anything that she touched. It was like trying to get something off the back of the top shelf at the grocery store, to get something that you couldn't quite reach. You could feel the tips of your fingers brushing against it, you could feel that it was there, you could try to stretch taller and taller, to get that last quarter inch that would let you finally grab hold of what you were looking for, but somehow, no matter how hard you stretched and turned and twisted, you could brush against your target but never quite get a grasp on it.

It was infuriating- exactly just like that kind of experience. It made you want to go and get a spiritual ladder or look for someone much taller in dreamwork who might be able to grab what you wanted and to reach it down to you.

And it was really beginning to bug her.

Instinctively, Morgan reached out with her mind, with her spirit to try to make a firmer connection with whatever crazy thing or dream that was trying to get through to her. To kick the TV or to jiggle the wire or to adjust the rabbit ears or to do what so ever it took to make the reception come in better.

Colors lights and sensations swirled more vigorously about her than before, to the point where she almost began to feel slightly motion sick.

Morgan set her jaw, metaphorically, kept reaching and tried her best not to get car sick while she did it

And then, for a moment, those eyes swirled back in to view again, those blue, blue eyes- and they widened, as if in surprise.

And Morgan sat right up wide awake in bed, her eyes widely open as well, heart racing, hyper-ventilating and hands clenched tight in the bedclothes.

"Those eyes" she thought, even as the images began to fade away out of her conscious mind. "Those bright blue eyes! I've seen those eyes before. Where have I seen those eyes before?"

She closed her eyes and tried to bring the image of those eyes back up but was only able to manage a few details before the whole experience started to melt away again.

She knew those eyes, but she could not think of from where, and the image had now become too fuzzy to help.

Well, damn.

"Well, let's just head back into sleep again." she thought. "Maybe I can get another quick peek and identify those eyes"

But try as she might, she was still so completely wound up that she couldn't get back to sleep. At all. No matter how she tossed and turned and tried and tried and tried.

And after a while, the darned little birds started at singing cheerfully and loudly outside her bedroom window and it was now time for another beautiful day to begin…

Chapter 9
Intuition

It'd been a very long day at work, but Morgan was finally heading for home. The thought of changing into her fuzzy slippers and reading a little bit before doing some yoga was singing the siren's song to her.

She saw the on ramp for the expressway up ahead and started to make her move right to get into the proper lane, but then she paused for an instant.

No. Not the expressway. Not tonight. She didn't know why, but she felt more like taking the surface route today, even though that route had far more lights and stop signs, took much more time and she was really, really, really motivated to get herself home.

"This isn't making any sense" she thought perplexedly.

But she took the surface route nonetheless.

And later that night, when she listened to the late evening news, she heard about the major accident involving seven cars and a tanker truck on the expressway that afternoon that had backed up traffic for hours and hours and hours.

She thought about that. Thought hard. Was there a reason that she happened to take a different route that day? Was this that inner wisdom Sam had spoken of kicking in?

Maybe.

She'd have to think more about that.

And later that night, Morgan went to bed and had another dream.

Chapter 10
Cold

Cold. So cold. So very cold. He was so very cold at the bottom of the oubliette, and, in the standing water, his feet were like paired blocks of solid ice.

They had dropped him in brazen chains into the bottom of a deep oubliette, almost 20 feet to the bottom. His feet were immersed in the half foot of water that had collected in the bottom of the "cell like a well", and the damp and the chill of the stony walls of the cell was sapping his strength.

As a swan knight, he habitually wore more armor than clothing, and the beatings they had given him during his capture and since had ripped away much of that so he had little in the line of garments to keep him warm. He curled in on himself as best he could, curling himself into a little ball as much as the chains would permit, trying his best to hold on to whatever warmth that he could possibly find left within him. His body ached with the cold and he just could not seem to get warm again, no matter how hard he tried.

The cold was eating him alive, biting down deep to the bone.

He huddled as best he could and then did his best to ignore his body, sending his mind out to warmer places.

He endured.

Chapter 11
A Cold Dream

Cold. So cold. So very cold. She was so very cold, and her feet were like little paired blocks of ice.

She reached out for her warm and wooly blue blanket but it seemed to have gone someplace else and she just couldn't find it with eyes still closed as they were. She felt around with her eyes shut for a minute, but it was just plain gone.

It was too much trouble to even try to find it, and the cold sucked away all of her strength, robbing her of any energy she needed to look for it. Giving up, she curled in on herself as best she could in the circumstances, curling herself into a tight little ball, trying her best to hold onto whatever warmth left within her. Her body ached with the cold and she just couldn't seem to get warm again, no matter how hard she tried.

The cold was eating her alive, biting down deep to the bone.

And then Morgan sat up in her bed, eyes wide. Her blanket was wrapped tight around her, and pulled up into a cozy hood over her head. The room was comfortably warm- even a little too warm, given the way that she had swaddled herself up in her bedding.

She was sweating profusely, and her body was slightly damp with sweat.

"Well, huh" she thought, as she untangled herself from her cocoon of bedding. "That was kinda odd."

But it was quite a while before she could get back to sleep again.

And when she did…

Chapter 12
Watched

He could feel that something was watching him.

He could not see what it was, not in the near total darkness of the oubliette, but he still knew that it was there none the less. He had that feeling, that funny / not so funny feeling, the one that you get when you are being observed by someone that you just have not spotted yet. That awful feeling of heightened alertness. The hairs standing up one by one on the back of your neck. The sheer knowing that you are being watched by someone or something even if you can not actually see by whom or what.

As a warrior, he had better senses than most folks had for detecting unseen watchers.

Something was watching him, and he could not see who or what it was yet. If history repeated itself, that would change later on. He had been through this kind of thing before.

This kind of thing had happened before. For the most part, they usually left him alone down there in the darkness. That was bad enough, but, sadly enough, not always the case. Sometimes they got bored and when the sidhe were bored, bad things happened. Really bad things. It would then be time to visit their prisoner in his dark and tiny prison cell and to find new and interesting ways to torment him.

To make him bleed just a bit.

His heart began to race. Combat was coming and he was unarmed and in chains. This was not a good thing. He had seen good things and they were not anything like this.

He started to breathe faster, but then he caught himself. He would send no signals at all to his hidden tormenters that he was afraid of them. He well might be their prisoner and totally at their mercy, but why should he give his captors any pleasure that he could avoid? He was not having any fun, so why should they?

He took a single deep breath then and, as best he could, consciously slowed his breathing patterns back down to his normal levels. Much better. A normal breath would relax his body and help him to be brave, and he would surely have need of all of the courage that he could muster right now and for the indefinite future.

He stopped and held his breath then. If he held still, held his breath and listened carefully, he could barely hear the sound of something breathing, something breathing high up on the walls above him. He did the best he could to locate by sound where that breathing was coming from. Knowing which direction an attack was coming from might spare him pain later on or even possibly save his life.

He casually, ever so casually, looked very carefully out of the corner of one eye and then the other, hoping to somehow catch a glimpse of something moving in the darkness. Sometimes, when you are being watched, you can alert the watcher to your awareness of him if you move too quickly and then really bad things can happen.

The sidhe were masters of Really Bad Things.

It was too dark. He just could not spot anything. And subtlety was not getting him anywhere. He turned his head slightly to one side and then the other, scanning a wider area of the tiny cell for the unseen spotter.

He still could not see anything at all, but an evil laugh came echoing down the well into the darkness of his prison. Someone or possibly something was evidently enjoying his discomfort.

His breath released with a whoosh, He could not hold it any longer, even to locate his tormenter. He started to turn more overtly now, swiveling his head widely from side to side, trying desperately to catch his unseen observer before it could conceal itself or launch an attack.

Whoever or whatever it was, it was quick, quick as lightning. He just could not catch it in the darkness, could not even catch a hint of movement out of the corner of his eye as he swung his head violently from side to side. His lungs heaved as his breathing speeded up again, unmindful of the impression he might be making on his tormentor. He tried to spin about, hoping that by covering a large area more quickly, he could finally find the unseen spy, but the chains and manacles would not permit that amount of movement and he crashed to a painful halt against the limitations imposed by his bonds.

Another evil laugh echoed downwards- and then a second one coming from a different direction above him. There was more than one of them. By the sound of it, something small, but malicious, and those could be the worst options when they came in packs. They tended to be the whipping boys of the unseelie, and so they had a lot of anger and frustration to work off when they were given the chance.

Something small but malicious moved above him, high above him on the walls of the oubliette and then he could feel something throwing itself down the shaft above him.

He braced himself to fight off all of the punishment that he was able to.

Chapter 13
Echoes

She could feel that something was watching her.

She couldn't see it, but she had that feeling that you get when you're being observed by someone that you've not spotted yet. The feeling of heightened alertness. The hairs standing up on the back of your neck. The pure knowing that you're being watched.

She froze, and then casually, so casually, looked carefully out of the corner of one eye and then the other. Sometimes, when you're being watched, you can scare the watcher off if you move too quickly and then you're left not knowing who has you under observation.

Nothing. Subtlety was not doing it, was not getting her anywhere. She turned her head slightly to one side and then the other, looking for the unseen spotter.

Still nothing but she could feel the watcher was still there, still watching her. So now she started at turning more overtly, swiveling her head from side to side, trying desperately to catch her unseen observer before it could conceal itself.

Whatever it was, it was quick, it was lightning quick. She couldn't catch it, couldn't even catch a hint of movement out of the corner of her eye as she swung her head violently from side to side. She tried to spin about, hoping that covering a large area more quickly would let her find the unseen spy, but something was keeping her from moving that much. She tried harder, wrenching at whatever was locking her in place.

And then she fell out of bed with a bump, pinioned once more by covers pulled tight around her limbs by her thrashing and turning in her sleep. The house shook with the vibration as she hit the floor hard, and she awoke suddenly, painfully, confused, disoriented and frightened.

Sam came running from the other room, and stood in the doorway as she lay there dazed.

"Are you ok, Morgan?" he asked.

She shook her head to clear it somewhat, but still a part of her was trapped in the dream. "I think so," she said, trying to stretch out her legs "but I think that I'm going to need some help to get out of these blankets…"

The cat smiled, relieved. "Your wish is my command" he grinned, and moved forwards to seize one end of a blanket in his mouth and tug at it.

"So, what's happening?" asked Sam, as they finished untangling her from her blankets. "Are you dreaming again?"

Morgan boosted herself back up on to the bed. "I think that I'm dreaming," she began "although I don't always remember all of what I've dreamed. I remember this one was scary, and it felt very real. It was almost like I was dreaming someone else's dream."

Sam tilted his head and thought about this for a moment. "Remember how I told you that dreams are often the way that your natural psychic ability can first begin surfacing?"

Morgan nodded.

"Well, there are a number of different ways that that can happen. Sometimes dreams are just your mind playing around while you're asleep. That's not psychic activity. It's just recreation."

"But sometimes, a dream can be symbolic. It can use symbols to let your psychic ability, your higher self or your guides and angels communicate with you. Sometimes a dream can be divinatory, and let you answer questions or find solutions that are important to you but that you can't solve with your waking five senses.

"And sometimes, a dream lets you travel astrally to another place or time to see or learn something you need to know."

"That makes sense," said Morgan "but I'm really not sure what kind of dreams I'm having, especially since I'm only remembering bits and pieces of them.

"It can be hard to figure out which kind of dream you're having, especially when you're just starting out and are new to all of this." said Sam. "Let me make a couple of suggestions on that."

"You might want to go by that new age store, Good Energy, tomorrow and get a reading to get some guidance on what's going on with your dreaming. And you might want to check there to see if there are any classes being held on dream work, to give you skills to deal with this."

"Sounds like a plan." said Morgan. "The sooner I can get a handle on this, the better. But for now, let me see if I can salvage what is left of the night."

"Good night then" said Sam "and sweet dreams to you, Morgan."

He slipped quietly from the room and she curled up in bed again.

And the rest of the night was quiet and dream free.

Chapter 14
Good Energy

The crystal wind chimes tinkled gently as Morgan pushed open the door to the Good Energy new age shop and walked in. Sarah looked up from her crocheting and then stood up to come around the counter and give Morgan the usual hug. She then pushed her out to arm's length and looked at her in some concern.

"It's nice to see you. Are you alright?" asked Sarah. "You look kind of run down."

"I've been having some problems sleeping lately." said Morgan. "Dreams…"

"Ah- then your intuition is coming in." said Sarah nodding briskly. "How can we then be of service to you, dear?"

"I'm looking for a tarot reading," said Morgan "but I'm afraid that I don't have an appointment now. Is he free?"

Sarah smiled. "For you, always," she said "but you just happen to have caught him at a good time. Imagine that. You can go on back."

Morgan headed towards the room for private readings that was at the back of the store, doing her best to avoid getting pulled into shopping through all of the wonderful items along the way. Crystals and knickknacks and books and recordings – the shopping was great here, but she had to focus on the primary reason she had come to Good Energy first.

She could always go shopping afterwards.

Reaching the curtained alcove at the back of the store, Morgan quietly called out "hello…" as a courtesy before she pulled the curtain back, to alert the tarot reader to

51

her presence.

The tarot reader looked up curiously as she came into the reading room. He was a tall and muscular man with long white hair, a beard and more than a little bit of 60s hippie in his manner.

"I'm sorry I didn't schedule with you in advance" she said "but I have a lot of things going on in my life and I'm getting the impression that some of them may be time sensitive or even urgent. It's disturbing and I'm looking for clarification on what's happening and what I need to do about it. Are you free to give me a tarot reading now?"

"I'm here and the cards are already warmed up." he said. "Take a seat and let's talk about what is going on."

She took a comfortable seat, laid her payment on the table, and did her best to organize her thoughts so that she could lay the issues out clearly and accurately. She knew she could save time and trouble if she thought about what she wanted to know so she could ask good questions and address things clearly– not because the tarot reader wouldn't understand her, but rather because being clear about what she wanted would help to focus the energies used in the tarot reading.

The problem wasn't that she couldn't get a decent reading here (she always did). The problem was more that she didn't really know what she wanted (other than a decent night's sleep, of course) and she had the feeling that, if she couldn't figure that out enough to ask a useful question, she might miss out on information that she'd wish she had later on.

"Well, alrighty then." she thought. "Give it your best shot."

Morgan took a single deep breath, centered herself and began.

"I've been having a lot of dreams lately," she said "and everyone's saying that it's because I'm beginning to get in touch with my intuition. They're probably right, but I've got a gut impression that it's something more than that- that I'm being sent some kind of information, that it's time-sensitive, and that, most frustrating of all, that I'm not hearing or understanding what I need to hear here."

"Part of the problem is that I don't usually remember my dreams. I'm improving but I can still only remember little bits and pieces, and that's making me crazy. The shortness of sleep I'm experiencing isn't helping either. It's making me cranky and clouding my judgement so, even if I do remember my dreams, I may still make bad decisions." she went on. "I've come to you for a reading and advice to help me straighten this all out, get a handle on this intuitive "talent" and make sense of it all."

"Can you help me?" she asked.

"Well, I can try." the tarot reader answered. "Let's start by breaking this down into smaller bites."

"First, I'm not surprised that you're beginning to experience psychic dreaming." he said. "With your increase in spiritual practices and your trips across the veil, it's what I'd expect to happen. It's one normal option."

Morgan felt a little better hearing that what was happening was frustrating but to be expected.

"You say that you didn't use to remember your dreams. Are you remembering your dreams now, Morgan?" he asked her.

"I never used to" said Morgan "but I find I'm starting to. Only bits and pieces, which is frustrating, but still more than nothing."

She thought a moment. "Come to think of it," she said "I'm getting the impression that I'm remembering more as time goes on. That's just an impression though."

The tarot reader nodded. "Impressions aren't facts per se but they're still worth paying attention to," he said "particularly in the psychic field where empathic input and impressions make up much of the information that you'll get. You should trust your gut. It sounds like one of the things you need to do is program yourself to remember your dreams. It sounds like you're already improving this on your own, but you may want some coaching on how to pick this skill up faster. You're taking the meditation classes held here, right?"

Morgan nodded. "It's teaching me a lot, but I'm not sure how that applies to remembering my dreams, though."

The tarot reader smiled. "It's a separate skill set from meditation, but fortunately the teacher also knows a lot about dreamwork, dream programming, remembering your dreams and lucid dreaming. If you wait til the end of class and ask her then, she can probably tell you enough to get you started working with this until you can take an actual class on dreamwork."

"Now let's identify the question for this reading. You say that you don't remember your dreams but that it feels like they're important and that you're feeling a sense of urgency about them. Is that correct?" he said.

Morgan thought and then nodded. That summed things up really nicely for her.

"So, let's look at the different kinds of dreams there are and try to narrow down what kind of dream you're experiencing. Once we've narrowed down what kind of dream it's likely to be, we can confirm and figure out what it's trying to do, which can help us shape a question for the reading itself." he continued. "First, do your dreams feel very real to you? Or do they feel goofy and fun?"

Morgan thought about that for a moment. "As far as I can remember, it doesn't actually feel fun. It's rather grim, actually. But it does feel very real to me, like I'm actually having an experience while I'm asleep."

"Well, that rules out simple mind play dreams, and makes symbolic dreams less likely. Does it feel like someone's trying to communicate directly with you?" said the tarot reader. "Is someone talking to you in your dreams?"

"I'm not sure." said Morgan. "A lot of it seems more like I'm an onlooker or sharing someone else's experience."

"So direct communication is less likely," the tarot reader said "and astral travel or clairvoyance seems more likely. Finally, you said that this felt like there was an urgency or time sensitive factor here, correct?"

Morgan nodded.

"So, it's less likely to be predictive (although it still might be) and more likely to be some kind of connection happening in real time." he said. "We'll have to keep in mind that all of this is theoretical, but at least it gives us a framework of more likely options and less likely ones to work with."

He picked up the cards and shuffled them, and then began to lay them out carefully on the table top.

"Let's start with a basic yes / no spread for each option." he said, dealing out rows of 5 cards in series on the table.

"Why are you doing that as opposed to using a pendulum?" asked Morgan. "And how do you do a yes / no tarot spread, anyway?"

"Well, I could use a pendulum," said the tarot reader "but, a yes / no spread with tarot cards can give me a little bit of additional info, and that can help us to figure out what to focus on. I'm using this method because my intuition tells me this is the right option to use in this situation. To do a yes

/ no spread with tarot cards, you choose a question or a topic, focus on your question or area of concern, deal out an odd number of cards and total up the points for how they fall. Upright cards count as yeses, reversed cards count as nos and the center card counts twice. We're going to use these quick yes / no runs for each option to narrow down what to target in the major reading as well as look for themes and information about each option."

He started flipping cards and carefully counting up each row.

"Random mental play – no. Symbolic imagery – also no. Predictive dreams – no, and no cards that indicate the future so definitely not the case here. Direct communication – no, not at the moment, but there's a card here that indicates you might start having that shortly in the future."

"But clairvoyance or astral travel seem much more likely in the here and now. I'm getting 5 out of 6 possible points for this option- so it seems like you're observing something that's happening currently but not being intentionally sent directly to you. It is like an old-time party line and you're just picking up the line on someone else's situation."

"And now that we have a feel for the situation, we're ready to start examining it in a bit more detail…"

Chapter 15
The Queen of Air and Darkness

And in the other world on the other side of the veil, a figure of power consulted the aethres and the calendar of the fates.

"Two more days." she mused. "Tonight, we ride. Tonight, we ride in and out and between the two worlds and tomorrow, we ride the same road as well and at the end of that, then the teind to hell is due."

"But fortunately, I have just the payment at hand…"

Chapter 16
Tarot

"Now, before we start on the reading itself, let's do a quick review of the basics of divination." said the tarot reader. "Do you remember what we've previously discussed about the nature of readings and free will?"

Morgan nodded. She had this one.

"You said that we all have the divine gift of free will, which means we have the ability to make choices and have a certain amount of control over our lives through those choices. Not total control but some at least." she said.

"You said that any good reading, by a competent, ethical and caring reader does not tell us about a locked in time and space future or doom, but rather about what's statistically most likely to happen if we keep doing what we're doing. You said that, if we don't like what a reading tells us, we always have the option to choose to change what we're doing, change the direction of our lives and head into a new and different future. You told me that this is one of the most valuable reasons to get a reading, especially on important topics and concerns, because it gives us more information so that we can make better, more informed choices."

The tarot reader beamed. "You obviously were listening, thank heavens." he said. "So many people don't, or don't remember. Now that we've gotten that nailed down, let's go on to the actual reading itself."

He gathered up the cards and shuffled them again.

"The question seems to me to be what are your dreams trying to tell you, what's happening, how will the information the dreams are trying to give you help you, and how can you best use that information to cope with that and cope well." he asked as he dealt out the cards on the table top. "Would that be the question that you want answered, Morgan?"

She thought that over for a minute. "Yes, that's right." she said. "I feel like something is coming fast and I want to be ready for it. I feel like the dreams are trying to tell me something and I want to understand them while the information is still useful to me."

"Then let's see what the cards have to say to us." said the tarot reader.

He picked up the first card in the row he'd dealt across the table top and looked closely at it before starting to talk. "The Star." he said, showing it to her. "Dreams and psychic input. Learning to adapt to new ways of experiencing things. Not really all that surprising a start, given the circumstances, but it tells us we're on the right track with the question that we've posed."

"The eight of cups reversed." he went on. "A blast from the past. Tying off loose ends. Revisiting situations that you thought were resolved but actually were not. Dealing with unfinished business."

Morgan thought about what past experiences might be coming back to bite her on the leg now. She couldn't think of any, not that she'd seen any sign of anyway.

"The tower." said the tarot reader. "Sudden violent change. You're in for another challenge and you'd best be prepared to move quick and keep moving. Whatever is coming is coming fast, but fortunately your dreams have given you a headsup and you're now more prepared to deal with it."

"Oh no. Not another learning experience." thought Morgan.

"Strength." he said. "You may be facing something

overwhelming and frightening, but you'll have the power and the control to do what you need to do. That's important to remember."

"The Three of Pentacles. Get help from the people you trust and work together to do what you need to do," he said. "and the seven of pentacles reversed – waiting for results that don't appear. Some of the people you trust will not be available to help you, but that doesn't mean they're not trustworthy. Some of things that you try may not work out quite the way that you expect them to, and that's worth keeping in mind. You may want to have a plan B on tap."

"The ace of swords and the ace of cups." he went on. "The beginning of a cycle of thought and research and the beginning of a cycle of intuition and emotion. Do your research and trust the established lore, but also trust your gut. Success will be based in a blend of intellect and of intuition."

"The knight of cups reversed. Not everyone who you encounter is who they appear to be, so listen to your inner wisdom and trust it when you're figuring out who's who."

"Temperance." said the tarot reader. "If at first you don't succeed, try, try again. And then once more. Repeating actions to gain the skills that you will need in order to succeed. Sometimes failure is a necessary part of the learning process."

"And, finally, Judgement. Undeniable change. No turning back. The choices that you make and the things that you do in the course of this sequence of situations will not only affect you in the here and now, but in the long range into the future as well. Make sure that you make good choices, or at least the best choices possible, and think about how they'll affect your present and your future before you act. You may not have much time to think things over and plan but take advantage of what time you do have."

"Looking at this time line here" the tarot reader said "I'm seeing a high proportion of major arcana. Five of them out of eleven cards. Having that high a proportion of major arcana tends to indicate that this is an important reading and is about major activities. Barely less than half so- not totally earth shaking, but still a major event or a series of major events."

"And on beyond the major arcana, half of the remaining cards are cups, which tells us that emotions, intuition and psychic phenomena will have a big effect on what happens. Once again, we could have guessed that, but it's good to have confirmation."

"It looks like you're heading for another big adventure, my dear" he said. "Do you have any questions about this reading or points that you need clarified?"

Morgan gulped and swallowed hard. "Er... Everything and nothing." she said. "Wow. It's intimidating and a lot to take in, and more than a little scary."

The tarot reader reached down and picked up the Strength card, and showed it to her again. It showed a beautiful woman opening the mouth of a lion. "Please remember though," he said "that, even if it feels scary, the cards say that even when things get challenging, you'll know what to do if you center yourself and listen to your inner wisdom. That you have what it takes to succeed. You just need to go with the flow- know when to act, know when to release and come together with other good souls who'll help you do what needs to be done."

"I've seen how you've adapted before when you faced outrageous challenges, and I'm sure that, if another challenge comes, you're up to the task."

"...but what if I'm not?" said Morgan anxiously.

"Why not ask yourself what if you are up to it? Why not tell yourself things that make you strong, as opposed to things that weaken you?" he asked calmly. "The more you focus on what you can do, the stronger you'll be."

"Have no fear, Morgan. You can do it. Trust yourself." he said.

She still felt a little bit wired, but she could feel her blood pressure dropping again. His confidence in her was contagious.

The tarot reader laid the strength card back down on the table and picked up the seven of pentacles reversed. "I find this one interesting, too- the one about waiting for reliable people who aren't available or things that don't work out as you had hoped." the tarot reader said.

""I know you said that people have been telling you that these dreams are your intuition becoming active. This is confirmation of that. Starting the day after tommorrow, the palmist and I'll be heading out to work at a renaissance faire many miles to the south, and I wouldn't have been available to work with you face to face as we did today if you'd waited to come in."

"Seems like your intuition kicked in to bring you by today to get the reading you needed."

"Keep in mind that we're available by phone to give you advice, but we won't be able to get to you in time if you need direct intervention." he said.

Morgan nodded. A reading in person was often more helpful and she was glad she'd been able to get her reading now, but it was still a little discouraging that one of her primary sources of help would be unavailable if she needed them.

It was interesting to see that her intuition was starting to be helpful to her though.

"Good luck and good fortune to you," said the tarot reader, clasping her hand "and please check in when I get back to let me know how things went."

Morgan nodded. "I hope things won't develop quite that fast, but I'll let you know what happens." she said, and slipped back through the curtain into the shop.

Chapter 17
Trapped

He stood alone there in the darkness, alone in a space too small to sit in or lie down in. Even if there had been enough space, the brazen manacles clamped to his wrists and the chain attached to the massive leather collar riveted tight around his throat would not have let him have that much freedom of movement or take that much ease.

And so he stood. Stood alone there in the darkness.

And sometimes the water seeped into his prison through the walls, pooling in the bottom of the oubliette and chilling him to the bone. It would have been a relief to be able to lift himself up out of the pool by the chains on his wrists, but there were also weighted brass manacles clamped onto his ankles, keeping him pinned down to a weight at the bottom of the shaft, his feet and his legs submerged.

At times, he was lucky and the dark and cloudy water only covered his feet and ankles, but sometimes it came up higher. There were a few times when the flooding almost touched his lower lip, and he had to keep his head tilted backwards at a precise angle to keep from going under and breathing in the foul water.

Sometimes he thought about letting go, tilting his head forwards and letting nature take its course. Only for an instant though, for despair was not the way of the swan warrior.

He could not escape.

He would not die.

And so he endured, alone in darkness.

Chapter 18
Trapped in Dreams

That night, Morgan fell asleep, and found herself standing in darkness, alone in a space too small to sit or lie down in. Even if she'd had enough space, the brazen manacles clamped to her wrists and the chain attached to a collar tight around her throat would not have let her have that much freedom of movement or take that much ease.

And so, she stood. Stood alone there in the darkness.

Water seeped into her prison through the walls, pooling in the bottom of the oubliette and chilling her to the bone. It would have been a relief to be able to lift herself up out of the pool by the chains on her wrists, but there were also weighted brass manacles clamped on to her ankles, keeping her pinned down to a weight at the bottom of the shaft, feet and legs submerged.

When she was lucky, the dark and cloudy water only covered her feet and ankles, but sometimes it came up higher. There were a few times when the flooding almost touched her lower lip, and she had to keep her head tilted back to keep from going under.

Sometimes she thought about letting go and tilting her head forwards and letting nature take its course. Only for an instant though.

She could not escape.

She would not die.

And so, she endured.

Chapter 19–
Reaching Out

He was not sure how long he had stood in the oubliette. With no access to day or night, and no cues to the passing of time, the days ran into one. He slept upright in his chains, leaning against the wall, and woke and slept again, growing weaker with time.

His mind reached out, trying to escape.

And then he made contact.

Morgan set bolt upright in bed, feeling tense and urgent.

"Those eyes!" she thought. "I know those eyes! Who is that?"

He lurched upright in his chains. "Those eyes!" he thought. "Those eyes I know! But who?"

And then the vision was gone.

And then the vision was gone. Morgan sat up in bed and concentrated on breathing deeply and slowly, and bringing herself back to center.

"What the heck was that about?" she thought.

Chapter 20
The Next Morning

Morgan dragged down the hall and into the cheerful kitchen, with bags underneath her eyes the size of suitcases for international travel. She passed by the place where the golden cat was holding court, sitting on the counter with a bagel with cream cheese and lox on an elegant bone china plate; and lunged towards the fridge where she kept an iced mocha ready to drink. Opening the refrigerator door, she seized the elixir of life and inhaled just over half of it, before turning to glare in the general direction of her furry and contented roommate

The cat looked up at her from the morning paper and met her glare with a deliberately mild and neutral expression.

"You're the first wave of the long-anticipated zombie apocalypse, I take it?" he asked her cheerfully. Morgan locked up and froze for a moment and then a reluctant grin slowly crept across her face.

"Caffeine…" she moaned ominously in a hollow sounding voice, and took another enormous slurp of her iced mocha before sitting gingerly down at a comfy wooden chair at the kitchen table.

She sat there staring glassily into space for a moment, sipping at the remains of her mocha before finally draining it. The cat looked back at the paper for a moment, glanced back at her with some concern, looked back at the paper again and finally gave it up as a bad job.

"More bad dreams?" he said sympathetically.

She groaned deeply, and tried to take another deep draught from the empty cup in her hand, losing track of the

71

fact that she had already drunk it down to the dregs. The sensation of "no mocha left" finally got through to the conscious parts of her mind. She blinked and then slammed the empty cup down on the table with a little cry of annoyance.

The cat very carefully looked away from her and began to groom himself. He delicately and thoroughly cleaned each paw in its turn, followed by each pointed ear, politely averting his eyes from her, carefully not staring at her and especially not smiling at her predicament. He himself had had certain mornings like this in the distant past (although he didn't choose to share them.)

Morgan opened her bloodshot eyes and glanced over at her roommate again, only to find him looking back at her both insightfully and implacably. She groaned deeply again and averted her eyes from him. She was so not ready for a discussion, any kind of discussion, right now and especially not any kind of discussion on a topic as far out as this one.

Maybe, just possibly she could find a way to duck the subject until she found and ingested enough caffeine, say maybe in about a couple of days-worth.

She looked back at him again. The cat was still looking at her in a sensitive, unblinking and irresistible force kind of way. She knew just what he was like when he looked like that.

"Arrr…" she groaned internally. "There is just no way to blow a conversation off when he's like this."

She peeked at him out of the corner of her eye. He was still looking at her. Still! She stared straight ahead again and just pretended not to notice.

There was a grinding, unpleasant sound at her elbow-

a kind of cross between a clearing of a throat and a clearing of a hair ball. Startled, she turned and looked at the cat full on.

He looked back seriously and compassionately. "I'm a cat and I can do this all day if I should need to" he said thoughtfully "History tells us that you won't be able to out-wait me; so why not get it over with now rather than prolong the struggle, my friend?"

"Let's just try this again, Morgan" he said calmly. He cocked his head most charmingly to the side, his eyes held open wide and his ears held at a particularly effective angle.

"More bad dreams?" he said sympathetically.

Morgan snorted and inhaled badly, resulting in a painful combination of laughing and choking. The golden cat leapt gracefully from the counter to perch on her shoulder, and, leaning over, pounded her vigorously on her back with his front paws while he balanced in position on her shoulders

"Bre-eathe!" he cried as he pounded on her back with his paws. "Breathe in. Breathe out. You know how to do this-I've seen you do it before!"

Morgan laughed harder and choked again.

Once the laughing and choking and purr-cussion had died down and Morgan was finally getting back to her regular breathing self, Sam leapt down from her shoulder on to the table in front of her. He put his front paws on her clavicles and stood up on his hind legs to look deeply into her eyes.

"Now spill it, Morgan." he said gently. "I know you were having disturbing dreams waking you up earlier last night and you have the look of someone whose night continued to go badly. What's up then, my friend?"

His golden eyes were inches from hers, inescapable and hypnotic. She was almost going cross eyed from looking into them.

She laughed "I give, I give!" she said "but it's not gonna help. It doesn't make any kind of sense at all. I keep having these dreams, very intensely real dreams, so very real that they're almost disturbing, but they come in flashes and impressions and nothing I can get a handle on. It's like the feeling that you get when someone's channel surfing a touch too fast for you to visually identify what you're looking at before you're on to the next thing, and who changes the channel over and over and over. That makes you cranky when it happens because your eyes never quite focus right and your mind can also never quite focus and make sense either before it's on to the next thing. You end up feeling over-stimulated and cranky– and what's worse is I'm getting sensory overload and overall crankiness in place of deep restful sleep I need so I'm actually getting a double dose of cranky. It's been going on for several weeks now and I'm just about at the end of my rope here."

"And, worse than that, I'm beginning to get a recurring theme here, but nothing so clear that I can make any sense out of it. The last couple of nights, I've been getting repeated glimpses of eyes, clear blue eyes like a deep, refreshing lake- and I could swear I know those eyes, I know them, but I just can't think of who they belong to. With all of the cranky and the tired and the overstimulated feeling, it's freaking driving me nuts!"

"Now I know you were saying something last night about this was only to be expected and it was a natural part of my learning things, but I'm so tired that I could break into tears, and I can't really remember exactly what you were saying either."

"So, tell me, what is it, Sam?" she blurted out. "Am I going crazy? What's happening here? Is something wrong with me? What's exactly going on?"

His eyes widened, and he snuggled his head past her chin and up across her neck. "Oh no, Morgan" he said, concerned "You're fine. This is just one normal way that people start tapping into their own psychic ability, and, given the number of things you've been doing to wake up your energetic abilities, I'm only surprised that it's taken this long for it to kick in."

He pulled his head back and looked deeply into her eyes once more. "I can see that we're way overdue to have "the talk" he said seriously.

She grinned weakly. "Is this talk the one that goes "when a mommy and a daddy love each other very much?" she asked "because, if so, I've had that one already…"

It was now Sam's turn to snort loudly. "Now don't get flip with me, missy" he mock snarled "because I know exactly where you sleep. Or don't sleep as the case may be…"

"Seriously, Morgan" he said, stepping out of her arms and back down on the table "we need to have a serious talk about psychic ability and you, and I think that it's way past time." He adjusted his position to classic cat pose; the position he used for all of his formal magickal mentor business, be it lecturing, proclaiming or making sure that she noticed how lucky she was to have such a very wise and attractive guardian in the magickal world.

"I don't know if every human in the world is psychic. All cats are, of course, but I'm not as sure about humans." he began. "I make the rounds but I haven't met everyone yet- but I believe that at least a majority of human beings have some degree of psychic ability, more or less. You see it in hunches and instincts and funny little things like knowing what song will be playing on the radio before you turn it on or thinking of someone you haven't talked to in a while and having them call you. That's all psychic perception- knowing things through senses other than the basic five. Unfortunately, people are told that psychic ability doesn't exist and so they've gotten very good at explaining it away again, rather than dealing with the fact that they're working the sixth sense.

"How much psychic ability people have and how much control they have over it depends on many factors, not only ones such as genetics and what their family gave them, but also what experiences in life they've had, and what they've done to try to develop and work with it. Someone who lives in an unsafe environment may become more sensitive and aware of danger from a psychic sense, because it keeps them safer. Someone who lives in a family where helping others is a family value may become more psychically empathic, because it supports the way that family interacts with the world. Someone who's raised by a family that believes in and accepts psychic ability and supports it will probably develop both a gift and the ability to control it and to make it stronger even sooner. It's like a muscle- the more that you work it, the stronger it gets."

Morgan was puzzled. "That's fine" she said, "but what does it have to do with the problems I've been having with sleeping?"

"Walk with me for a bit." said Sam "We're getting there in stages."

"As if that were not enough complication," the golden cat went on "in current society, there's bias against psychic phenomena of any type. You may see it in movies and on tv, but the average American is socialized to deny the existence of any magick or psychic ability at all, and will leap through enormous hoops of flaming logic to explain away any experience that challenges that particular belief pattern. This is one of the reasons that magickal creatures, including cats, can walk unseen in modern society if they so choose to do so and that the Lands that Lie between can pop in and out of connection with this world without exciting more comment. It's because people don't want to notice it and will do their best not to if confronted with it."

Morgan did a quick mental inventory of some of the experiences she'd had since she'd moved here and slowly nodded her head. "That would certainly explain a lot." she said thoughtfully.

"And when it comes to the question of having or of developing psychic or magickal abilities themselves, most people will fight like maniacs to keep from acknowledging it, unless they have some kind of social support that believes in the psychic or the magickal. If not, they'll just about stand on their heads to come up with "rational" or "reasonable" explanations for their experiences that are neither rational nor reasonable." said the cat.

Morgan was struck for a moment by the irony of getting a lecture on people in denial about the nature of psychic phenomena and magick from the fuzzy lips of a talking cat.

Oblivious to what she was thinking about, Sam went on. "People have and will always come up with a lot of really good reasons for why they can't possibly be psychic." he said ironically. "Things like "oh that's just silly" or "how could I even know that?" to things like "There is no such thing as psychic ability." Or "who are you to think you're special enough to be psychic?" They'll even believe that, if you're psychic, people will think that you're weird and won't want to be around you, and, out of fear, they'll unconsciously block their own psychic ability so they don't get rejected by their friends and families."

"And that's how dreaming becomes important." said the cat meaningfully.

"You see, when you're awake" said the cat "your conscious mind is in control, and one of the important parts of your conscious mind is your judgment."

"Now judgment gets a bad rap. People will tell you not to be judgmental, but when it's used right, the way it's supposed to be used, good judgment is there to keep you from doing stupid things, like touching that hot stove or going on a date with that person who's already threatened you with harm. The trouble with judgment is when it tries to keep you safe based on inaccurate beliefs, like "If I'm psychic, people will think I'm weird and reject me, so, since I want friendship and love, I can't be psychic so I reject it."

"But, on the other hand, when you're sleeping" the cat went on "your conscious mind (including the judgment that tries to keep you out of trouble by blocking anything that might make you stand out) is also asleep- but the unconscious mind is still awake; and the unconscious mind is very powerful. It has a majority of the power of the brain, including the mind body connection. It has a majority of the untrained and unconscious psychic and magickal ability. And it doesn't have judgment spoiling your fun, and holding it back from things you can do that the conscious mind and judgment does not want to admit you can."

"This's why" said the golden cat "for a majority of human beings (as opposed to cats who are perfect and don't go through the denial phase), the way that psychic ability first surfaces is in the form of dreams. because when you're asleep, judgment is not around to tell you "You can't do that!"

"So you do it. You just plain do it…"

"You dream. There are different types of dreams, of course, and not all of them are psychic. Some of them are just fun. Some are responses to physical conditions, like dreaming you're a seal pup on an ice flow and waking to find all of your covers on the floor, or having indigestion and dreaming you're a pot-bellied stove. Some are your brain working overtime, trying to sort out an experience or question from your day."

"But some of them are psychic. Some are seeing things that are happening at the present moment in a different place than the one where our body is sleeping. Some are getting snippets of the past, or of the future. Some are dreams that let you access your own psychic wisdom to get answers to questions or useful information that you or someone else needs. They all can be very helpful once you've learned how to understand and work with your dreams, and they can create a bridge that helps you to eventually learn how to access your abilities when you're awake."

"There's a whole lot more to this than I'm saying at the moment, but this gives you the basics of what may be happening in your dreams that keeps waking you up, and why it's happening now." Sam said "You've been spending increased amounts of time walking in magickal worlds and hanging out with magickal people. You've been learning to access your inner wisdom by using a pendulum. You've been developing more mental control through meditation. You've been beginning to build the energy in your body through chi gung. You're moving your energy and your consciousness in a direction of more awareness, more strength and more control, and evidently the powers that be have decided that you're ready for a new and bigger psychic skill set."

Morgan stared at him. "Sam, are you saying what I think you're saying? Are you saying that the reason that I'm so sleep deprived that I'm just about hallucinating is that the universe is upgrading my super powers? That it's like the psychic version of the browser on my laptop?" she snapped. "Well, that would explain why I can't make it work and why it keeps breaking down on me."

Sam reached out one velvet paw and patted her face gently with it. "It's just a temporary annoyance, my friend" he said softly. "As you get more experience and control, you'll also be able to make more sense of the information you're getting and get better sleep again."

Morgan made an unhappy face at him. "Well, as an effective teaching method, that really sucks big time." she said. "So just how do I get this wonderful experience and control? Can you teach me the things I need to know? Is there some kind of basic manual like "Psychic Dreaming

101" that I can get? Do I just have to wait it out, and hope that I don't go round the bend from sleep deprivation in the meantime?"

The golden cat looked thoughtful. "I can teach you some of it," he said "but if you want to get a jump on dream programming and better use and control of your psychic dreams more quickly, I'd recommend that you talk to the teacher running the class on meditation you're going to. She's really well informed on brain waves, altered states and the mind body connection, and probably knows more of the tricks you need as a human to get a handle on this faster. We cats are born knowing how to walk in both the dreaming and the waking world, but you humans need training to fully make the most of the difference."

"Or, you can just wait it out." Sam said "You're a smart woman and you've proven yourself to be adaptable, so my best bet is that, with sufficient time, you can pick this up on your own."

Morgan thought about that and made an unhappy face. She wasn't comfortable with the idea of a short ration of sleep for an indefinite time. Beyond that, there was just something else niggling at her that gave her a vague sense of urgency and anxiety. It was as if, if she couldn't sort this all out pretty soon, it'd be way too late for something important. It was like this psychic dreaming was not just coming in now because it was the next logical step in her personal development, but rather because there was some kind of need coming that needed to be met, like the universe had decided that she was the most convenient tool at hand for the job and was adjusting her to fit it.

"You know, it sounds self-important," she thought

"But it also it feels like that's what's really happening here. Everyone I've talked to has said that I need to learn to trust my instincts and my intuition. Maybe I just need to trust it here now, even if it does sound like I'm puffing myself up a little."

"No, I think I need to get working on this" she said to her furry roommate. "The idea of living on next to no sleep for who knows how long is not one I'm willing to go with here. I'm bad enough after a few bad nights. I can't see going for months of them until things settle down."

"I'm also getting the impression that time is of the essence and that I need to get moving on this as soon as possible. Thank heavens that my meditation class is tomorrow night- I'll have the chance to touch base with my teacher then and maybe she can give me more tricks for getting in the driver's seat of my dreams. In the meantime, can you get me started with anything that you know about how to work with this?"

"As always, it'll be my pleasure to do so" said Sam "but first, before we start, if you could just fix me another bagel with cream cheese and lox to fortify the inner feline? And you might want to have one too, my girl. After all, fish is brain food, you know."

She grinned at the golden cat on her lap and then carefully reached around him to pull open the refrigerator and to take out the makings for her first breakfast and his second, before they dove into the intricacies of dream work. Lessons always went better with food,

Or at least Sam thought so.

"It's good to remember that psychic dreams come in a variety of types" said Sam as she sliced the bagels and spread the cream cheese across them "Some are literal visions of things that are actually happening, or have already happened or are going to happen. Others are more symbolic. In those, one thing will stand for another and you have to figure out what the things you're seeing actually mean."

She layered the salmon high on each of their bagels and set his plate down gently in front of him. "Ooo beautiful salmon" he said and class stopped for just a moment before going on, while he took his first bite and made yummy sounds.

Chapter 21
Learning about Dreaming

"… and you're feeling very relaxed now and very healthy and positively wonderful, but now it is time to come back again, to come back to your bodies, to return from that beautiful place of energy and relaxation and back into your everyday life, to bring that feeling of energy and relaxation back with you, to carry it with you throughout your day and through every day from now on."

Morgan felt herself gradually drifting back towards a conscious state again. The teacher was right- that did feel fantastic and she did feel both energized and relaxed.

"And now, as I count up from 1 to ten, you will feel yourself becoming more awake and alert and come back to your body."

(She was getting so much better at this meditation thing. That rocked!)

"1, coming back now, coming back now."
"2 becoming more aware of the room around you."

(…And it was so good for learning the ability to focus her intent better…)

"3 coming back now coming back now."
"4 becoming more aware of your breathing."

(…When she thought of where she was when she started out, just a few classes ago…)

"5 coming back now coming back now."
"6 becoming more aware of your body."

(...*it was truly amazing how far she had come...*)

"7 coming back now coming back now."
"8 stirring and stretching."

(...*She was going to have to expand her own meditation practice outside of class...*)

"9 almost completely back to us now."
"And 10, wide awake, wide awake, wide awake, alert and aware, fully back in your body feeling great, energized and relaxed, whole and healthy and ready for a great evening."

(...*It would make her life so much better in so many ways.*)

Morgan opened her eyes and stretched her arms and her legs luxuriously. She was surprised at how, after a relatively few sessions, she was really getting into this meditation thing and how good she was getting at it. The class was offering a number of different types of meditation too. She was beginning to find out which ones worked best for her, and use them more frequently at home in between classes.

The sounds of her classmates around her also returning to normal consciousness, stretching and shifting made her smile. She wasn't the only one this was really good for.

"All right, folks" said the teacher, switching off the background recording "Anybody got any thoughts? Anybody got any questions?"

She waited for a moment.

"All right then. Next week, we'll be doing a walking meditation so be sure to wear comfortable shoes. See you all next week then."

People began to bustle about, pack up their things and go. Morgan hesitated for a bit. She wanted to catch her teacher after class and talk to her about the dreams that she'd been having but she didn't want to talk about this in front of the other students. She'd sound crazy to people who hadn't had the kind of experiences that she had. She also wasn't sure if this was a good time for her teacher and she didn't want to presume about that.

Her teacher noticed her waiting there. She made eye contact with her from the front of the room. "Anything up with you, Morgan?" she called, as she continued to coil the extension cord on the boom box.

Morgan paused and then walked slowly, hesitantly up to her teacher. "Have you got a moment?" she said quietly. "I've got some questions about something that's been going on in my life lately and I need some answers. I've been thinking about it, and I can't think of anyone besides you who'd be qualified to tell me what I need to know."

Her teacher blinked at her once, and then again, and then grinned slightly at her. "Well, that's a pretty big lead up to a question" she said, as she quickly slipped the meditation CD into her side pocket "Perhaps I should be intimidated here. I guess I'm kinda flattered that you thought of me; but we'll wait and see about that until we finally get to the actual question. So, what's happening?"

She sat down in a handy chair and gestured for Morgan to get comfortable as well.

Morgan shifted uncomfortably from one foot to another and remained standing.

"Well… erm… it's just that I have been having, well… dreams... and… well… they seem so real to me." she said.

Her teacher raised an eyebrow.

Morgan listened to what she had just said and blushed. "Oh, not that kind of dream…" she said.

Her teacher's grin grew wider then. "Oh," she said cheerfully "so that's it. You've gotten to the stage of developing your intuition then."

She patted the comfortable chair next to her invitingly "Sit down, honey. This is something to be expected. Since you're learning more about your intuition and about walking with one foot on the magickal side of the fence and one foot in our world, it was only a matter of time until you got this far. It's a natural part of the process, my dear, and nothing to really worry about."

Morgan still felt anxious but also relaxed just a bit. If her teacher already knew about this sort of thing, maybe it wasn't quite as big a deal as she'd thought.

"It's getting rather disturbing at this point" she said, finally seating herself next to her teacher. "The dreams are so vivid and feel so real that I've been waking up in the middle of the night repeatedly. I'm having a hard time getting enough sleep, and the impressions that I'm getting are somewhat frightening. It feels real and kinda spooky. It's like hearing someone I know yelling in the other room, but not being able to hear what they're saying. Frankly, it's creeping me out."

Her teacher leaned slightly forward in her chair and listened more seriously now.

"I'm getting the impression" Morgan said flatly "that there's some kind of message I'm supposed to get here, but I just can't seem to get it. I can't hear what I'm supposed to hear. I can't learn what I'm supposed to learn, even when I half hear it over and over. And I don't know how to ask for a clearer message."

"As if that weren't enough, it feels like time's running out for me to get the message and to figure out what they're trying to tell me." she added "And that's just scaring the life out of me."

"So what kinds of dreams are you having?" said her teacher. "Ones that feel real until you wake up? Ones about things that happen the following day? Ones that feel like someone is talking to you?"

"The dreams feel very real" said Morgan hesitantly 'and the sheer "real-ness" of them sticks with me for quite a while after I wake up. They're hard to get out of my head. They don't seem to predict anything, but I can't tell that for certain. And they're really kinda fragmented- I feel like I'm looking at flashes of something or someone but I don't get the full picture, or even enough to make any sense of it at all."

"And, given the obnoxious way that it's messing with my sleep patterns, it'd be nice to at least get something useful out of it." she said, finding herself suddenly angry.

"Hmmm. Important information but not predictive dreams and not direct communication dreams, eh? Rather dreams about something happening in the present and information the universe feels is important for you to know," said her teacher thoughtfully. "And you're only getting quick flashes, not full images?"

Morgan nodded, vaguely reassured by this. It sounded like her dreams fell into some kind of pattern, and if there was a pattern, perhaps there was a way to get control somehow and maybe sleep well again. Maybe even learn something useful here.

"Has anyone talked to you about how dreams can connect with psychic ability?" asked her teacher. "How, for many of us, the first place that our psychic ability breaks through is in our dreams. Because, in our dreams, our conscious mind isn't awake and our judgment therefore isn't ready to tell us all of the sad and bogus little reasons why we can't possibly be psychic?"

"Just a little bit." said Morgan "Sam told me a little bit about that- but if I'd known that it'd be so frustrating, annoying and exhausting, I think I'd have returned the whole darned psychic package, thank you very much."

The teacher smiled sympathetically. "It's just a problem for you right now because you're in the awkward in–between phase. You get enough input to make you restless but not enough to be interesting or useful to you. That's not a fun stage at all. You need to work on getting some more control of it, so you can make use of it rather than just have it run over the top of you."

"So exactly how do I do that?" Morgan asked.

The teacher thought about that for a moment. "Has

anybody talked to you about intention yet?" she finally asked Morgan

"Not really." said Morgan "What's intention?"

"Let's start with metaphysical basics." the teacher said. "When you break metaphysics down to its simplest level, it's all about energy and what we do with it. It's about creating it, about moving it and about using it to accomplish something." said her teacher.

"And, in metaphysics, an "intention" is just a plain old, fancy-schmancy, new-age way of saying "goal" and "setting an intention" is simply setting a goal for what you're going to do with the energy you're working with."

"Now, connecting to this," she went on "there's a principle called the Law of Attraction, which says that whatever you give most of your time, your resources, your attention, and your energy to is what you will get more of. Where attention goes, energy flows, and by setting our attention on the things that we want as opposed to the things that we don't want, we also set the vibration of our own energy fields. We set our vibration and we attract more of what we are we are focusing on. We attract not only more of what we are focusing on, but also more of other things that vibrate at the same frequency."

"As an example," her teacher said "if I spend a lot of my time focusing on the unpleasant person who lives next door, not only will I find that she comes over more frequently, but also that I start getting more unexpected bills. Contrarywise, if I spend more time reading books about helpful people, not only will I find more helpful people coming into my life but also unexpected windfalls and chocolate chip cookies. Are you with me so far on this?"

Morgan sat and thought about this for a moment. She remembered the conversations in her kitchen about this with Ariella, Estelle and Sam. While the concepts seemed unusual, she was beginning to see how they might work and also spot examples from experiences she'd had in her own life where the Law of Attraction might have been hard at work.

"OK" she said hesitantly. "I think I can see how that might happen, although I'm not quite sure yet if I'm ready to embrace the concept with open arms. But how does this concept apply to my current situation, the one with the out of control psychic dreams?"

Her teacher smiled at her. "It's actually pretty simple when you think about it from that standpoint." she said. "You're spending more time walking in magickal worlds and hanging out with magickal beings, so that's attracting more magick into your life. You're learning how to tap into your own intuition and psychic ability more, so you're attracting more psychic ability into your life. You're learning more practices that help you to create, work with and focus energy, and you're giving your time to practicing them, so you're drawing more energy into your life- and it has to go somewhere, you know."

Morgan gaped at her for a split second and then slammed her hand against her forehead. D'oh! She'd had every one of the pieces and she still hadn't put them all together like that without a friend to walk her through all of it step by step.

"Don't feel too bad." her teacher grinned. "This is all very new to you, and it takes time and experience before you start to see the new patterns these processes make in your life. Be gentle with yourself. You'll get there."

Morgan sat still and processed these ideas. She was beginning to see the pattern of how this fit together, but she needed more information.

"I can see how that may explain why psychic dreams are coming into my life now and making me crazy," she said thoughtfully "but that's still only half of the picture here. That explains why the dreams are here now- but what do I do to get control of them- both so I that can get useful information out of them and so I can actually get a good night's sleep again?"

"It's actually a combination of two principles- intention and the law of attraction." the teacher told her. "First you use the Law of Attraction to set your own vibrational level and gather energy, and after that, you set an intention about what you want to do with that energy."

"In this case, you set your intention about remembering your dreams in a clear way that's easy for you to understand."

Morgan knit her brow. She could see there was an answer there, but she still needed more information to make it work for her. "So how do I do that?" she asked "I see the point but I'm still not quite getting how I do this."

"Two good ways of doing this are positive self-talk and affirmations." said her teacher. "Self-talk is the stories we tell ourselves about the world around us. Many times, we block our psychic abilities by telling ourselves that we aren't psychic. If you watch what you tell yourself, whether out loud or in your head, and catch yourself when you tell yourself something negative, you can correct that by telling yourself something positive like "I can remember my dreams."

"And affirmations are quick positive statements that you repeat multiple times to replace beliefs that don't support you with ones that do. You can repeat them out loud or write them down. Studies find that repeating an affirmation 1000 times can change your beliefs and the behavior based on them."

"Last, one of the best ways of getting control of your dreams is dream programming." continued her teacher. "Every night that you want to dream true, as you go off to sleep, tell yourself silently or out loud something like "Tonight I'll dream and dream true, and in the morning, I'll awake, renewed and refreshed, I'll remember my dreams in a form easy to interpret and I'll know exactly what my dreams are trying to tell me."

"And every night that you just want to sleep," added her teacher "as you go off to sleep, tell yourself silently or out loud "Tonight I'll enjoy deep and uninterrupted sleep, uninterrupted save only for such information as is key for my safety and well- being, and that of those I love." That's to keep you from ending up on every dreaming chat forum out there."

"Dream programming may work the first time or it may take multiple times, but if you keep practicing, you'll find you have more control of your dreams and working with them. Is that enough for now?" asked her teacher. "Is that enough to deal with your problem and get you started at working on this?"

Morgan thought. This was a lot of information, and she could tell already there was a lot more that she'd have to learn, but she was already feeling more hopeful.

"Yes, I think that's enough for now," she said. "and thanks for walking me through this."

The teacher leaned over and patted her hand. "It can be pretty disconcerting when you first start having these kinds of dreams" she said kindly "but in time, you get better control over your dreaming so you can use it to access your psychic ability, get answers to questions that you can't answer in other ways, visit places you have never been, and do a lot of other cool and useful things."

"Right now, you're in the middle of your growing pains, but start working with your dreams and you'll grow right past that stage. You just wait and see." said her teacher

Morgan smiled, relaxed and stood up again. "I'll have to try programming tonight and see what happens." she said.

"Well, let me know how it goes" said her teacher, also standing "and if you need any coaching, you know where to find me."

"That I do." said Morgan, as they walked towards the door leading out of the classroom together.

Chapter 22
Intentional Dreaming

That night, Morgan lay down in a comfortable position, arms and legs uncrossed, and ran herself through a full body relaxation, starting at her toes and working upwards through all of the parts of her body. As the different parts relaxed, she could feel her mind relax as well, and feel it usher her downwards into sweet and welcome slumber.

Once her body was fully and completely relaxed, and she was in a half–awake/ half –asleep Alpha brain wave state, like the one she experienced when doing visualization in meditation class, she began to slowly give her unconscious mind some suggestions.

"Tonight, when I sleep…" thought Morgan drowsily "I'll dream a significant dream, one that gives me information important to my immediate future. Tomorrow, when I wake again, I'll be able to clearly remember my dreams and easily understand what they mean."

She mentally repeated the same suggestion to herself, over and over again, until at last, she gently dropped off to sleep.

And that very night, Morgan dreamed– and she dreamed true. And the next day, when she awoke, she remembered her dream.

Chapter 23
Contact

Morgan dreamed she was hovering in a dark, damp prison.

She was not alone. She was floating in the air over a slumping figure weighed down with chains and despair.

She couldn't recognize the person at first, so she "pushed" with her will and forced herself to drift closer.

And then the figure startled and turned and she found herself looking into familiar blue eyes.

"It's Claud!" she thought "but he's dead, isn't he?"

Chapter 24
Claud

Claud jerked in his chains, his mind filling with the sight of startled grey eyes.

"It's Claud!" he heard, "but he's dead, isn't he?"

It could not be real. It must be an illusion. His mind was falling apart from the dark and the imprisonment.

But it still felt so real...

He focused his will and pushed out, secretly terrified lest he lost contact.

"Not dead. Not dead. Not dead." he thought. "By the trooping sidhe, imprisoned."

And then the connection was ripped away...

Chapter 25
Checking Her Facts

Morgan sat bold upright in bed, a vision of blue eyes still caught in her mind.

"That was Claud!!" she thought "and he's alive!! Held captive but alive!!"

But as she woke up, her conscious mind came more into focus, and, with that, came her judgement.

"...But what if I'm just kidding myself?" she thought slowly "dreaming of things I want that aren't actually true?"

She sat for a moment, and then lunged for her purse at the end of the bed.

"Wait. I know how to check this." she thought, pulling out her pendulum. "Instead of doubting myself, I can check for accuracy."

"Pendulum' she thought "was I dreaming?"

The pendulum swung up and down, indicating yes.

That was discouraging. Morgan thought a moment and then asked "Was I communicating through my dreams?"

Once again, the pendulum said yes.

Morgan took a deep breath. "Is Claud alive?" she asked, hopeful and frightened at once.

The pendulum said yes

"Was I communicating with him through my dreams?"

And the pendulum said yes one more time.

She'd been working with her pendulum for awhile now and had learned that the answers it gave were accurate as long as she asked good questions.

She'd learned to trust it.

"Sam!" Morgan shouted "Come here! I've got big news!"

Chapter 26
Burd Janet and young Tam Lin

Later in the day, the swan maidens were back, hearing all about Morgan's dreams.

"So a dream that Claud alive is you had?" said Ariella skeptically. "Unlikely to me it sounds …"

"No, no, these things can happen." said Estelle.

"I checked it with my pendulum." said Morgan. "This was evidently a bit of astral connection through dreams. He's being held prisoner by someone known as the trooping sidhe."

"There's precedent for this." said Sam. "The sidhe have a history of stealing mortals they desire, whether as nursemaids, bards or attractive people of either sex. The trooping sidhe gather energy and power by trooping, which is processing along certain paths at specific times. One particular story pertaining to that is the story of Burd Janet and young Tam Lin."

"It was long ago and far away" started Sam, in the rhythmic tones of a storyteller "when the age was darker, and the sidhe more powerful, and humankind walked in humility and in fear. In those days, magick didn't lie hidden in the world one breath apart from the one we live in now. In those days, Magick walked openly in the world, brave and brazen; and the only thing that one could be sure of was that anything was possible."

"and that was often not a good thing…"

"Now, in those days, the sidhe were more powerful than they are now, and they strode the world openly, taking whatsoever they desired; and humans hid from the unknown

105

behind locked doors, raging fires, cold iron, and such prayers and charms as were given to them."

"In particular, the unseelie sidhe were both proud and covetous, and would help themselves to whatever struck their fancy, be it a fine horse, or a pretty trinket, or a pile of gold."

"Or a human being, of course. The sidhe were known to often take people that they wanted for their own use. They particularly preferred children, or pretty young women, or handsome young men, or those with a special gift, be they fiddler, or seer, or bard. They would seize a person and take them away, all willy-nilly, whether that person wished to go or nay."

"And sometime they treated them well, until at last they tired of them. And sometimes they took them away purely for the pleasure of tormenting them. For the sidhe find their pleasure in different pastimes than you and I."

"And the story rarely ended well for unwilling guests of the sidhe."

"Now, there was in those days, a woman called Burd Janet; and she was with child by her sweetheart, who was called young Tam Lin. But alas, her love had been stolen away by the Queen of Elf Land and bound by magick to ride in her elven train, for he was fair to look on, and the Queen had seen him once and lost her heart."

"Bird Janet?" asked Ariella. "Vat kind of bird? A swan she vas, then?"

"Hssh!" hissed Estelle. "Qviet be! The cat, an important story is trying us here to tell ..."

"Vell, to know this I vant." insisted Ariella. "The difference between if she a pelican or a vooping crane may important be, no?'"

"She's not a bird!" said Sam. "She's called Burd Janet because, back in the day, the Scottish term for woman was "Bird' or "Burd". And now, ladies, may I continue?"

The two swan maidens blushed. "Yes." they said in unison.

"Now many a maid in that day and that situation would have lost her will, and done nothing more than simply sit and bemoan her fate most pitifully;" the cat continued "But Burd Janet was made of stronger stuff, and was resolved that her child should have a name and that she should have her true love back, if even the hordes of hell should block her way."

"Burd Janet went unto Carterhaugh, the lands that had been left in her keeping by her father, and the place where she last had seen young Tam Lin, her lover; and there, by the side of a certain enchanted well, she plucked two roses, one red as blood and one black as night."

"Leaning over the surface of the waters, she stirred them with each bloom in turn, and then gently surrendered them to the waters."

"And, as if in a dream, the face of her own true love appeared to her in the waters of the well."

"The Queen of Air and Darkness has captured me and holds me captive." said the vision. "And only you can set me free. In three days, the Dark Queen and her elven train will ride, and I, as her thrall, shall be compelled to ride with them."

"They shall troop along the paths long established to gather the magick cast by the turning of moon and stars, and I shall ride as one with them. If you should wait hidden along their path and pull me from my horse as we pass by, and hold to me no matter what occurs, you might save me and free me and return me to the halls of men."

"If aught I do can save you" said Burd Janet "then that thing shall be done. Our sweet babe needs a father, and I need you back safe with me."

"They will try to wrest me from thee." said her true love's face. "They will turn me into other things, things to startle you, things to frighten you, things to harm you, all to make you loose your hold on me. But you must not – for if you let me go for but a second, I'm lost to you, and you shall see me no more."

"I stand advised, my love," Burd Janet said "and I shall not release you, no matter what they change you to. Our dear babe and I need you back."

"You must hold fast to me, no matter what changes they make in me" said young Tam Lin "until at last I become a naked man– myself with naught of my own to bring with me. Then you must throw your cloak over me, and bring me home with you, for you will have released me from the Dark Queen's thrall."

"A naked man? Uff da!" giggled Ariella, elbowing Morgan. "Yah, at dat point in the game, she had better vell her cloak over him throw."

"You shuush!" scolded Estelle "The story line, you are breaking up, you!"

"Ahem" said the golden cat, looking at them both severely. "Your lives and limbs may well depend on the knowledge in this tale. Do you still want to hear the story or not?"

"Yes, Sam." they both said, abashed.

"Now, when the sidhe do ride," the cat continued "you may not know me when you see me. They may cast a faerie glamour on me to make it hard to find me. If so, remember this– they will have me on the white horse closest to the town. They do this in recognition of the knight that I once was, and by this you shall know me."

"Burd Janet said "Then their tricks shall not deceive me, nor their threats afright me, nor their glamours keep thee from me til I hold you in my arms once more."

"And the image smiled, and faded into the waters of the well."

And late that night, as cold winds blew and wolves howled and all reasonable people were home in bed, Burd Janet crept from her home, all wrapped in her heavy woolen cloak. She traveled over hill and dale and broad, dark highway until at last she came to the edge of the path that marked the procession of the elven troop's rhading."

"And there, behind a bit of bracken, Burd Janet hid herself on the town side of the path under the dark of the moon."

"And soon, and soon, and soon again," crooned the cat "she heard a noise there in the darkness– a jingling as of horse's harnesses in the distance. And, far away down the path, she saw a great light coming towards her."

"Burd Janet caught her breath, and made herself as small as possible. In a moment, the light came around the curve in the path, and the elven procession was upon her."

"First there came a noble herald, bright and shining, laying the way for the elven rhade and preparing the path for the noble beings yet to follow. Next there came a mass of hunters bearing torches and a phalanx of the younger elven knights all in full comparison, their armor gleaming in the reflected torchlight. And following them, a cluster of both fair and merry maidens, gaily comparisoned in bright and shining silks and satins, the trappings of their steeds decorated all about with tiny bells of silver and of gold."

"And then at last, amidst a cluster of more seasoned knights and of elevated nobles of every ranking mounted on steeds of every color, there rode the Queen of Air and Darkness."

"Her hair was scarlet, and flowed like silk." said the cat "Her skin was pale and bright as moonlight on a darkling night. Her eyes were deep and shining, full of ancient knowledge, and brightly lit from within by awful power carried deep within her. She was dressed all in flowing cloth of crimson, from her throat down to her instep, and the train of her gown dragged softly upon the ground as her horse stepped prettily along the moonlit path."

"And as the procession passed along the paths appointed, the bushes parted and Burd Janet stepped forth, bold and fearless, upon the path of the trooping sidhe. Horses startled, hounds howled, and elven knights drew their swords and spurred steeds towards her."

"Without a word, Burd Janet dashed to the knight on the steed of white closest to the sleeping town, and reached up to grasp him by the leg and pull him down off his horse. Face concealed by helmet, the pale knight fell heavily, and lay immobile upon the sward."

"Burd Janet threw herself to the ground and seized the fallen knight tightly within her arms. "You shall not have him!" she said, turning to face the Elven Queen in the moonlight. "You shall not have him! Young Tam Lin is my own true love and the father of my own bairn, and none but I shall have him."

"The Unseelie Queen looked darkly down on her, a faint smile upon her lips, as Burd Janet knelt upon the moonlit sward."

"Is that so? Well, you may keep what you can hold, my dear– no more and no less" said the Queen and gestured slightly only once."

"And young Tam Lin groaned deeply once within Burd Janet's arms, and began to thrash about. As he writhed and bucked and struggled, his armor fell away and a wild and savage fur sprang up to take its place. He howled aloud with a fierce and desperate voice, a voice both man and beast."

"And Burd Janet found she held within her arms not a man but rather a massive wolf, strong and violent, with candle glaring eyes and massive fangs that clashed together within inches of her throat."

"And Burd Janet quailed for but a moment, with powerful jaws gnashing fiercely at her, and then, gathering her spirit, clung tightly to her love, dropping her head to her breast to shield her throat and face."

"The wolf fought full fiercely, but Burd Janet held on more fiercely still, amidst the clashing of jaws and howling. Then all noise ceased, and Burd Janet heard the Unseelie Elven Queen laugh quietly once."

"And the love within her arms changed again."

"The fur, so quickly sprouted, fell more quickly away, leaving a smooth and slippery skin, difficult to hold, sliding away beneath her grasp. Her lover both dwindled and grew, becoming thinner and longer. With a vicious hiss, his head swiveled impossibly about, and she saw that he was now a monstrous adder, with dripping fangs and a length so wrapped about her that it was difficult to determine who was holding whom."

"The massive adder thrashed and swiveled, and brought its head about to press its face full close to hers. Deep luminous eyes gazed into Burd Janet's, staring through all her defenses to see the fears that lay within her. Its fangs brushed against her cheek, and it opened its gaping maw."

"Burd Janet shrieked involuntarily, and all the elven train laughed scornfully, like the sound of wicked silver bells. She shrieked with fear– and then took a firmer hold on her writhing, threatening captive; wrenching her body around so her shoulder was presented to the adder's mouth, as opposed to her vulnerable face and throat. She threw herself over hard on the ground, with the adder's head beneath her so her own body's weight became a weapon to stun the serpent, and dissuade him from wickedness."

"The adder thrashed for a moment. An unnatural cry burst from its throat, and then it slacked and lay limp in Burd Janet's grasp, her arms and legs still wrapped firmly about it. And the sidhe stopped laughing."

"The sidhe were serious now, no longer laughing– save only their Queen, whose too perfect features still held that ironic half smile. She looked down from on high on her perfect steed – down at Burd Janet, rolling about on the ground, covered with dirt and leaves and a considerable length of snake, with her hair all askew and a smudge on her cheek."

"And she smiled unpleasantly, and gestured one more time."

112

"One more time, one final transformation, and the shape within her arms and legs was transformed once more. Cold and scaley skin became warm beneath her grasp, and then hotter and hotter. It burst into flames and burned away from her love. Her captive shrieked with pain as he became a burning figure, wreathed in crackling flames. Heat radiated off him in massive waves that hit like a blow from a giant's fist. The flames against her body scorched her clothes, singed her skin, and made it difficult for Burd Janet to breathe through all the smoke and flame."

"And all of the court of the trooping Sidhe sat there by moonlight and watched in silence, even the Queen."

"and Burd Janet sprang to her feet with a piercing shriek, still holding fast to her true love, though he scorched her hands and face; and she ran with haste from the elven track, her love caught tight within her grip, ran down the bank that led to the gleaming loch below them. And, reaching the banks of the loch, she plunged him briskly into the shining waters, and herself with him, still holding fast to the prize that she had given so much to win."

"And a great cloud of steam arose from off of the cooling waters, and, in her injured hands, the figure transformed one final time; and Byrd Janet found herself holding her own young Tam Lin, as naked as the day he was born, and fainting in the waters beside her. Burd Janet threw her cloak over her fainting lord, and caught her baby's father close beside her."

"Burd Janet looked up from the loch where she stood hip deep in the water, supporting her love. She looked up to the gleaming elven pathway on the bern high above her. And she saw there the elven folk, in all of their enchanted glory, looking curiously down at her and at what was now hers. For a moment, her heart quailed within her."

"And the elven queen stared full horribly at her for just a moment, stared at her with her dark and ancient eyes. And then she smiled coldly, nodded her head but once, and then rode on then with all of her fine and shining people with her. For in this world, there are the greater laws and rules, even for those who are impossibly great and dark and powerful; and what was won fairly, could not be unwon."

"And Burd Janet clasped young Tam Lin closer," said the golden cat "and took him home with her, home to be her husband true and the father of the bairn that slept within her."

"And that" Sam said, shaking his head in order to break it clear of the story "is the tale of Burd Janet and how she reclaimed her love young Tam Lin from the keeping of the trooping sidhe, and their dark and powerful Queen."

"The end." the golden cat said, and very casually began to wash one paw.

"If they want to keep this young Tam Lin as their prisoner," asked Morgan "why do they take him out riding around the countryside? It just seems like asking for trouble to me."

Ariella's brows knit for a minute, and then she brightened.

"To show him off it probably vas, yah?" she said with satisfaction. "A favorite outfit did you ever have? In the closet, it didn't stay hidden, did it? No, on you put it and around the countryside pranced so vat pretty things you had they can all see, yes?"

"You're probably right" said Morgan "but we're still

going to have to rescue him. Who can we get to help us?"

"Vell, on the other end of the county our flock are, in var games engaging." said Estelle. "Interested ve vere not, so to visit you ve came."

"And there's not enough time to cross through the gates and bring back support from the seelie court before the trooping fae ride." said Sam.

"And the palmist and tarot reader are off at a ren faire down south," said Morgan "so all they can do is consult by phone."

"I guess it's just us" she said "so we'd better get ready.'

Chapter 27
Preparing

Morgan dowsed and re-dowsed to determine the path the fae would take, so the rescue party could choose when and where they'd intercept them.

Sam dug out a bottle of herbal spray they could spritz on themselves to hide themselves from any unseelie hounds that ran with the rhade.

Estelle poured over the variations of the ballad of Burd Janet and True Thomas, to pick up any information that might be helpful in their rescue.

And Ariella pulled out cloaks for the three women from their closets, because all of the ballads said that cloaks would be needed.

And the clock kept ticking.

"It's time." Sam said finally.

Chapter 28
The Trooping Fae

It was a damp, dark night, despite the cool shimmer of the moon shining down on them. Several hours of rigorous pendulum dowsing, with multiple double-blind questions thrown in, had given them the path the fae would follow. They knew by tradition the nights the trooping fae would ride were the three nights of the full moon, but they didn't know the time the troop would pass. They crouched in prickly underbrush in the gully on the path side closest to town, legs cramping, body chilling and damp creeping into their shoes as time slowly passed.

Ariella sneezed loudly, and then sneezed again.

"Hush!" said Estelle. "Everything you vill spoil! You vill let them know that here in the bushes ve are hiding!"

"Vell, it I can not help." complained Ariella. "In these bushes is something making me sneeze. No fun at all this foolishness is. Hope I only can that for all ve are enduring Claud vill grateful be."

Her sister glared at her, and made the "I'm watching you" hand gesture. Ariella glared back at her and fiercely bared her teeth.

Morgan grinned at the both of them, and then caught her breath sharply as an overtaxed muscle cramped. "They don't talk about sneezing, bickering and leg cramps when they tell the story of adventures." she thought. She started to mentally count backwards from a hundred and shift slightly to one side to ease the pain in her leg.

"Hush" said Sam softly. "Someone's coming . . ."

In the distance around a bend in the causeway, they

119

could see a gleam of uncanny light and hear a distant jingle of harness and echo of voices approaching. Still glaring at each other with lips clamped shut, the sisters froze. Morgan caught her breath and watched for the approaching faerie train.

They saw the light coming closer and heard a chiming of voices like small silver bells. Then the first of the trooping fairies swung around a bend in the path, and the court was upon them.

First, riding out before the rest, came a herald in brilliant satin livery, mounted upon a golden horse. In his hand, he bore a shining horn that he blew upon repeatedly as he processed to announce the progress of the court that followed.

Next, rode grooms, huntsmen and lesser servants of the court, lower in stature but all bedecked in finery fit for any mortal noble. Falconers rode with birds perched on fist, goshawks and merlins and peregrines, each according to the glory of its owner.

Following them, a group of lesser knights, clustered in formation to provide protection to higher folk that followed. Each lesser knight was clad in the colors and device of his master and each one bore a lady's favor upon his belt or tucked into his helmet. Every knight rode upon a curveting horse with fiery eyes with bells braided into its mane. There were horses of black and of white, of gold and of brown and of gray, and each one minced down the path in an exaggerated gait, its hooves stepping high as it pranced upon its' way.

A cluster of bright and shining ladies followed after, laughing and chattering to one another as they rode. Silk and satin shone in the enchanted light, but not as brightly as their flowing hair and shining faces as they rode in the elven train, flanked by elven knights. Silver bells jingled on their ankles and depended from the caparisons of their high stepping palfreys.

A skillful minstrel in parti-colored clothing rode in close attendance on the ladies, his lute in hand, strumming and singing bright and cheerful songs of love as he rode.

Hounds, bratchetts and retrievers of all shapes, sizes and colors ran back and forth along the length of the procession, whining eagerly or stopping dead at a sharp command from an elven master. Each dog was a perfect example of his breed in looks, manner and comportment, and not a flaw could be found amongst them. There were even a few dark hunds that ran loose amongst the rest of them, although other members of the pack tended to give them a wide margin of space when permitted by their masters or the huntsmen, who cracked their whips to call the pack to order.

"I'm so glad that we thought to use herbal sprays to mask our scent tonight" thought Morgan "or else the dogs would have surely scented us by now. If not for that, we'd already be in trouble here."

And then, at last, came the greater knights, each a dark champion in his own right. Lances were held at ease and swords at the ready, prepared to defend their ruler if there was a threat.

Their ruler, yes. Their Queen. And there, there in the heart of the trooping elven rhade she rode, the Queen of Air and Darkness, beautiful and fiery and dangerous, seated high upon an ivory steed

She had skin as pale as moonlight and long hair as

red as blood. Her hair was caught up a series of intricate twists and braidings, woven in and out of itself in a pattern that seemed to move and shift and alter itself in the moonlight in patterns that seemed to mean something dark and dire. She had eyes, dark eyes, eyes that shone with mysteries and promises and screams. She was tall and lean, beautiful and deadly, queen of this unseelie elven host.

There was air of peril about her as she rode. Not just one of dangers known, although certainly of that as well, but also of hazards and risks that one had never thought of, ones not created until this very moment.

Morgan and Ariella and Estelle pressed themselves flatter into the gully, doing their best to avoid any royal attention until it was time to act.

Bright silver bells jingled and sweet music played and the sound of merry laughter and melodic voices in conversation rang out as the trooping sidhe rode on their way. Unearthly light shone out through velvety darkness, marking the passing of a train both breathtakingly beautiful and incredibly dangerous.

The members of the rescue party crouched lower behind the bushes below the verge, pressing their bodies close to the ground and holding their breaths to keep from being heard. Bright eyes shone and then pressed half closed, trying to see what passed while not being seen themselves. Morgan looked first to the left and then to the right, moving her eyes only but not her head, to check on her companions without moving enough to draw attention to them.

Ariella stretched out on her right, tight to the earth but muscles tensed, ready to act when the time was right. Estelle lay flat to her left, taking advantage of any cover she could find, eyes searching for anything that could be of help to them. Morgan couldn't spot Sam, but given both his status as an enchanted creature and his own natural cat-tish nature, he'd only be seen if he wished to be, so the fact that she couldn't see him was no surprise.

One of the hounds ran by along the road's verge above them. He stopped short, sniffing carefully at the air, ears pricked and alert. Morgan thought she'd been holding her breath before, but found she'd been mistaken. Her breath became more shallow than shallow. Morgan found herself concentrating hard on being nothing, on being transparent, on not being there at all. "Not here, not here, not here." she thought, clearing her mind of any other thoughts.

The scenting dog paused a moment. It sniffed the air once more, almost thoughtfully.

"Brutus, heel!" one of the elven huntsmen cried out sharply, and the scenting dog's head snapped quickly about. "Brutus, come to heel! Come away, now, you base and naughty cur."

The dog whined quietly. Its ears went down flat and its tail tucked ever so slightly between its legs, and then it backed away, slowly at first and then whirling about and diving back into the pack.

Morgan eased out a breath frozen tight in her throat, and forced her tightened fingers to relax their death grip on the grasses she lay on. "How were they going to be able to seize Claud and bear him safely away," she thought "if the mere thought of being discovered by one of their smaller dogs was enough to immobilize me?"

The elven herald passed by them on the road above them, and then the falconers, the grooms and the servants.

The lesser knights rode by them next, their armor shining brightly in the enchanted light, and the elven ladies fair, beautiful, well defended by their men at arms and with their human minstrel close in tow.

Morgan crouched down in the underbrush, muscles tense and mind racing. "How are we going to do this?" she thought. "We have to find Claud and reclaim him from the unseelie sidhe, but how will only three women and a talking cat stand up against a full rhade of trooping fae? This seems impossible."

And then she caught a sudden rush of movement to her right.

And all questions suddenly became academic

"To the infernal regions vith all of this" swore Ariella under her breath as she pushed to her feet and dashed up the hill and out of the gully. She'd evidently gotten tired of waiting to act. She burst out of the bracken surrounding the gully they were hiding in and leapt up the slope to the road up above them.

"That fool!" thought Morgan franticly, scrabbling wildly in the bracken and trying desperately to get to her feet. "She couldn't wait! It's way too soon! We're supposed to take them from behind!" She grabbed at the underbrush, reaching for any possible handhold to pull herself upright and get her moving up the slope behind Ariella. She could hear Estelle struggling likewise to come upright and get moving up the hill behind her sister.

"I was going to use my seeing eye to see through any glamours or illusions they may have set up." thought Morgan wildly as she lunged up the hill after the impulsive swan princess. "And now she's going in glamour-blind, and anything could happen to her! Why couldn't she wait for a couple of minutes more, when we'd have the best chance of success? Why couldn't she act with the team for once, and keep the small advantage we get from surprising them?"

In keeping with traditional tales about this sort of situation, they'd hidden themselves off the road on the side closest to town. Tradition held that the captive knight would be unrecognizable because his helm's faceplate would be closed, but that he'd be riding on a white horse on the side of the road closest to the town, in recognition of the status given him within the trooping fae; and that such a knight could therefore be found by any person loving or desperate enough to risk the ire of the unseelie by trying to reclaim her loved one.

As both a swan maiden and a warrior born and raised, Ariella had better reflexes and was faster than most humans could ever dream of being. She was up and out of the ditch, onto the road, and in amidst the sidhe before any of them could even react to her coming. She stood for an instant on the edge of the road, taking her bearings now that she had a better look at the entire troop. Elven dogs alerted and bayed, falcons mantled and displayed their wings in alarm, horses bugled loudly and helmeted heads quickly snapped around, targeting on the unexpected threat.

The knight on the white horse was several mounts back from where the swan maiden stood. She spotted him and was off like a shot, weaving swiftly in and out of startled horses, avoiding the snapping teeth of alarmed dogs and taking advantage of whatever cover she could find from other knights just beginning to draw their swords or to swing their lances in her direction.

She reached the nervous white horse that was prancing and starting to go up on its hind legs. It shied away from her and fought against its rider's hands on the reins. Speeding up, she ran straight at the massive horse and, as she reached it, leapt up and onto its back, throwing her arms about its armored rider and knocking him off of the broad back of his ivory mount. They both fell heavily to the ground on the far side of the massive animal, her arms and legs clasped tightly around her target. The horse rose up high on its hind legs in alarm and then dropped heavily back down again, striking out with heavy hooves as they rolled beneath him in the shadows on the ground.

They had both hit hard, with Ariella thankfully on top. The impact knocked the wind out of her for a moment, dazzling her and making her dizzy; but still she held on tightly to the figure clasped securely in her arms.

"Tight I must hold." she thought "No matter what should next happen, the secret to the rescue is tight to him to hold. Just to tight on hang…"

She clung harder to the figure in her arms and waited for the trials that she knew would come next.

At that point, the armored figure wrapped his arms tightly about her as well.

The stallion was still moving above them, plunging, bugling and kicking out in all directions. An elven groom leaped in and grabbed the reins of the agitated white stallion, by raw strength alone pulling him away from the pair on the ground, leaving them exposed to the eyes of the other sidhe. Elven knights gathered around them, high on horseback, holding their mounts firmly in check and looking down at them with eyes of flame, and at last there came the Queen of

Air and Darkness herself, beautiful and powerful and perilous.

The queen looked down from on high at Ariella where she lay on the ground, and Ariella looked back up at her with apprehensive but resolute eyes and a determined chin.

Then the unseelie queen smiled- and it was not a pleasant smile at all

And then the Queen of Air and Darkness gestured imperiously.

She gestured just once.

And then everything changed…

And not at all for the better…

Ariella suddenly found herself frozen in place, immobile and unable to move so much as an eyelid. Below her, from where they were clambering out of the gully, Morgan and Estelle also dropped heavily to the ground, caught by the power of the Queen and unable to move, although thankfully still unseen or perceived by the sidhe.

The arms that had wrapped firmly around Ariella now clamped down on her in a painful grip. The figure's legs also locked around the recumbent swan maiden, pinning her in the damp and the dirt.

And the helmet melted away, leaving her nose to nose with a nightmare face, topped with a scarlet hat. Large and ill proportioned, like a killer jack-o-lantern. Two huge eyes, staring fiercely deep into hers, brimming with spite and malice. A broad and animalistic nose and a far too wide mouth that stretched around the sides of the head, looking as if it was meant to open more widely than any natural mouth could gape.

What mouth would possibly need to be that big? And what purpose would such a massive maw serve?

Startled and a bit afraid, Ariella gasped but held on firmly.

And then she remembered what she was here for, and smiled with renewed confidence. "All a part of the test it is." she thought. "On I must hold." And she clasped her companion closer.

His lips parted slightly, and a stink of death and decay wafted between them. A hint of teeth, too many teeth flashed between the lips.

"All a part of the test it is." she thought more frantically. "On I must hold. A part of the test it is. On I must keep holding."

The nightmare face grinned open mouthed at her and showed her a maw full of needle teeth like a shark. It stuck out its tongue and waggled it at her lasciviously. It gnashed its pointed teeth at her, and then, without warning, lunged forwards and sunk its pointed teeth where the curve of her swan like neck met the arch of her shoulder, biting down hard into the tender muscle there.

Ariella screamed aloud from the pain but did the best that she could that she could to keep holding on. "Just a trick it is. All just a dirty unseelie trick it is." she thought. "Only an illusion -but so bad it hurts?"

Her partner gnawed ferociously at her as they lay in the dirt, and after that one scream, Ariella bit her lip and remained silent, not wishing to give the sidhe the pleasure of her pain.

The Unseelie Queen looked down at her from high on her horse. "No, my dear" she said ever so ironically "It is not an illusion. Not at all an illusion."

Ariella stared up at her, wide eyed both with pain and with surprise. It was like the unseelie queen could read her mind. Could she do that?

"You silly, silly, silly little thing." said the queen, "It takes no great feat of magick for one such as I to know what you are thinking. I have ridden this same road many times before, and you, my dear, are nothing new. For thousands of years, we have ridden these hills, and for thousands of years we have taken any beings as we have desired. For thousands of years, we have also faced those who would try to reclaim our lawful prey."

"Did you think for a moment, my dear, that we are stupid?" said the unearthly queen "That we are to be fooled by the same old trick on each occasion? Do you think that we have learned nothing, nothing at all, in all of that long time that we have been riding?"

A cold and awful feeling came over Ariella. She knew that this was supposed to be a test for her, but she was getting the frightening impression that this was not the test she had studied for…

"You have come, my dear, with the somewhat vague idea that if you follow the old tales, that if you are brave and pure and loving, that if you seize your own true love and hold tight to him regardless of what illusions and trials I may put upon you, that you will eventually triumph overall and bring about some sickly kind of happily ever after story."

"But you know, my dear, the world is not at all like that." said the queen. "It is not that simple. The starting point of any heroic quest is to choose your target wisely, lest you be trapped in a nightmare of your own making. And you, my dear, you have chosen very poorly indeed." said the queen scornfully. "In your youth and your ignorance, you thought you knew exactly what you wanted but, in truth, you did not know at all. The one that you were seeking was not the one you chose. We have him in a place far safer than that and a little harder to find. Instead, my dear, you have chosen the red cap, who is one of my most faithful of servants, and as his reward, he shall have the pleasure of teaching you the error you have made in trying to steal from me what is rightfully mine."

Her beautiful eyes narrowed to slits. "There shall be lessons…" she said softly "There shall be lessons… and you shall surely learn better."

The Queen of Air and Darkness smiled darkly. She then turned away from her new captive and towards her unseelie troop, with a flamboyant gesture that encompassed them all.

"And now, my loyal fairie folk, enough of these small pleasures for the moment." the Queen cried out loudly "Let us instead be away and on our road again! Let us complete our journey, hasten on to our destination, and take our ease therein."

The red cap grinned fiercely then and slowly released his teeth from Ariella's shoulder; pulling her roughly to her feet, still faint and bleeding from her wound. A groom brought up a dapple gelding and the red cap threw Ariella roughly up on to it, still half fainting from shock and from loss of blood, mounting behind her to hold her captive. The groom pulled the white stallion away, still shying and bugling.

And the whole troop rode on.

And as the sound of horses and of bells and of cruel elven laughter faded gradually into the distance, something in the air relaxed and slowly, painfully, Morgan and Estelle found they were able to move again. They curled into themselves on the ground from the awkward positions they had fallen in, curling up and finding their centers again before stretching out and trying to work feeling back into their fingers and their toes once more.

And as they reconnected with their bodies, they also at last reconnected with their minds- and with the current situation as it really was.

Ariella was gone. She was really gone. And she was gone under the worst of all possible circumstances. A prisoner of the Unseelie Fey- and not for the first time.

They hadn't gained a prisoner- they had lost a swan princess.

Estelle stared at Morgan, eyes widening with realization and horror. "Mein gott. Mein sister I have just lost." she whispered. "Me mein mama is gonna kill."

And, long after the trooping train and the unearthly light were gone, there was a long and shocked silence in the ditch.

"Well, that didn't go nearly as well as I'd have hoped." said Sam.

Morgan and Estelle both turned as one and looked at him. Hard.

"What?" said the cat.

Chapter 29 –
Regrouping

The three of them remained crouched half the way down the gully, looking at each other with stricken eyes.

"Gone mein sister is ..." whispered Estelle "and as well, Claud."

"We did everything right" said Sam confusedly. "This should have worked. Why didn't it work?"

"And now they have two of our friends captive, as opposed to one." said Morgan.

They stared blankly at each other for a moment; and then Morgan's jaw tightened.

"We evidently didn't have the whole story" she said. "We need answers, and we're not getting them here. We need to go where the answers are."

"Right." said Sam. "To the library then!"

Chapter 30
Research

They'd reached the library, where there was light, protection and plenty of references, metaphysical or otherwise. As usual in cases like this, Morgan had smuggled Sam into the library inside of her purse amidst complaints about the barbarity of a civilization that didn't permit superior beings, such as cats, access to the halls of knowledge. Now she, cat and Estelle were safely forted up in the carrels in the back upstairs.

Estelle was still distressed by her sister's capture but, belonging to an enchanted, migratory, and barbarian culture, hadn't actually spent much time in the library before. The towering shelves of knowledge as far as she could see temporarily distracted her from her current situation. "Ooo, at all of the beautiful books look." she gasped in awe, scanning "and full of mystical knowledge they all are?" Part of her mind was still worrying about Ariella but part was already calculating the possibilities available and trying to figure out how she could apply for a library card when she had no fixed address.

"Nope. Sorry about that, Estelle." said Sam, carefully licking one paw to turn the next page "Some of them are about other interesting things like container gardening, or classic movies from the golden age of Hollywood, or the latest pop idols. Now let's get back to work and do some research. Time's passing fast and we don't have much time left if we're going to rescue Claud and your sister. Many traditional sources list an open window of three days when the prisoners ride with the trooping fairies and we've already burned through one."

Morgan staggered back into the carrels, arms piled high with stacks of books. "Here's more references on the trooping fae," she said, dumping one stack in a cubicle with a thump "and over here," she said, heavily dropping another stack "we have books that reference human beings stolen by the fae and ways people have gotten them back again. Did you know there are over a dozen versions of the tale of young Tam Lane and Burd Janet alone? Sometimes he's a human being who's been stolen away by the Sidhe, and sometimes he's a Sidhe himself who's dallied with Burd Janet. And her name isn't always Burd Janet either…"

Estelle bit her lip as she flipped quickly through the books in front of her looking for something useful. "Er… Morgan…You know that not altogether human Ariella is, right? For that matter, neither Claud is. From human beings originally ve are descended but over the years the magick has us changed so partly human and partly something else ve are. Both members of the MantelFiedervolk, the Swan people, they are and neither true humans at all, strictly speaking."

"That's true- but the swan folk are still partly human and the principles of the story true for humans long ago still should hold true as well." said Sam, fixated on the thick volume in front of him. "The point is that they're sentient beings stolen away by the trooping fae because of qualities the sidhe found desirable, such as being virgins, or minstrels, or knights, or pregnant women, or midwives, or bards, or just plain old attractive people."

"Damnation!" he shouted, frustrated. "There are too many answers and not quite enough at the same time! If only we could figure out what we did wrong, we might have a fighting chance at getting them back again, and maybe even coming out of this alive. My fur's way too pretty to trim an elven collar."

"Ssh, Sam." hissed Morgan. "Remember we're in a library now, and they have rules about shouting. We really don't want to rouse the…"

"Ahem." came a quiet, firm voice behind her.

"…the librarian hearth spirit…" said Morgan quietly, eyes cast down. "Well, hello there, Mary. Sorry about all the noise."

"It'll not be happening again." she added quietly, but with an edge to her voice, while giving her golden cat the Look.

There was the sound of a throat clearing. Morgan slowly turned around and looked at a testy hearth spirit and resident librarian. Mary's hair was long and dark, caught back in a professional hair-do combining the best points of beauty and utility. She was compact but not short, fit but not emaciated, dressed in a casual grey tweed jacket and skirt, feet shod in comfortable flats and her deep grey eyes partially hidden behind horn-rimmed spectacles. Those eyes were glaring a bit now, and the foot tapping ever so slightly as she stared at the overly loud cat.

Caught in the cross fire between the librarian's rising ire and his roommate's frosty glare, the ebullient cat became slightly more subdued. "Sorry." said the golden cat, his head dropped and his tail tucking between his legs.

Morgan and Mary both glared at him for a moment more, and then the hearth spirit chuckled slightly. "Well don't do it again, Sam" Mary smiled. "Bad enough that we have someone getting loud in the library, but if they find out there's a cat here, there'll be no end to system restructuring. If you want to keep coming here, you need to keep your cool and behave yourself, so no one finds out. Keep your doggoned voice down, my friend."

The golden cat grinned and looked a little bit relieved. "Really sorry about that, Mary, but it's so frustrating to be doing research but not be able to find any clear answers. J. R. R. Tolkien said "go not to the Elves for counsel, for they will say both no and yes." and I'm starting to think the same thing about traditional tales. I was hoping for answers and all I keep getting is more questions!"

Morgan gave the golden cat one more sharp look and then turned back to the pile of books she'd just put down. Estelle turned another page and kept reading.

"Exactly what kind of answers are you having problems finding?" asked Mary, reference librarian side intrigued in spite of herself.

"We're looking at all of the literature we can find on trooping fairies, humans stolen away by them and how to get them back." said Morgan, eyes firmly locked on the book she'd just opened. "We've got a situation here, and not much time left to sort it out."

Startled understanding bloomed in Mary's eyes. "I see," she said tensely "and who's gone missing, my dears?"

"First, a warrior of the Mantelfiedervolk that we thought had died earlier this year" said Morgan, eyes still racing across the pages as she answered the librarian.

"...but then mein sister vent the hero fool to play and now captive by the trooping fairy folk she has also been taken." blurted Estelle, reminded that her sister was gone.

"Ve do not know if back again her ve can get."

Her tears began to flow and she threw herself at Morgan, research all but forgotten in her misery.

Startled, Morgan looked up from her book at the sobbing swan maiden leaning on her. "How is it that I always end up being the mature comforter?" she thought slightly crankily "and how can she cry like that without getting red eyes and a snuffly nose anyway? If I cried like that, I'd look like a mess in 5 minutes, but swan maidens look beautiful and delicate no matter how hard they cry. Must be some kind of super power like that other one that they have- the ability to pass unseen when they so choose."

She carefully and gingerly put one arm around Estelle, and held her gently as the swan maiden wept. "There, there, there." she said, feeling uncertain about the whole thing in general.

Sam had no uncertain left in his make up at all. "I know you feel bad, Estelle," he said "but we need you to hang tough and to get back to reading again. Time's short now and we need all the answers we can get if we're going to get Ariella and Claud back."

Estelle sat up once again, her pale face covered with tears but still beautiful. "This I know" she said, snuffling sweetly "and brave I vill be. All that I can do I vill do to help the answers ve need to find." A few more tears leaked softly from the corner of her eyes and trickled down her pale and porcelain cheek, but the swan shaman took a deep breath and bent over the reference books once more in a determined fashion.

Sam turned another page and scanned the new one quickly. "We just need to figure out exactly where we went wrong" he muttered under his breath. "We followed the traditional tales exactly. We hid and we waited while the majority of the elven train rode by. We chose the knight on the white horse closest to the town, just as in the traditional tales. Ariella certainly took them by surprise and seized the knight on the designated white horse and, having been clothing shopping with her, when that girl grabs hold, there's no getting her to let go, so that part was perfect."

"So why did it go so terribly wrong? We should be sitting comfortably in the kitchen at home, laughing, telling tales and cleaning out Morgan's fridge, not here in the library, cursing fate and scrambling through tons of reading material, searching frantically for a clue of what to do to salvage the situation before it's too late."

"Don't forget what the elven queen said to Ariella while we were all frozen." said Morgan, one finger in the air but eyes still firmly locked on the page in front of her. "She said "We have been riding the hills like this for thousands of years. Do you think that we have learned nothing at all in all of the time that we have been riding?"

"That means that, even if we research all the traditional tales and follow them exactly, there may still be some changes in the basic formula here."

There was sudden silence, heavy with the sound of a change in mental direction. Sam stopped dead, and then turned to look at his roommate, abandoning the page he was reading. A look of horror spread across his furry face as the implications of this opened up in his mind.

"Oh dog crap!" he exploded. "You're right, Morgan! That means this research may not have anything to do with what's happening now or in the next couple of days; and that there's no good way to figure out what we did wrong or how to get Claud and Ariella free again from the trooping fairies! What the heck are we going to do then? It's hopeless!"

Estelle's dark eyes began to fill with glistening tears again. She looked ready to break down once more in counterpoint to Sam's emotional explosion. Mary took a deep breath and began to raise one admonishing librarian finger, sympathetic to their problem but ready to bring them both back in keeping with appropriate library behavior.

Morgan looked around her at her fellows, half panicked for just a moment, and then took charge.

"No, no, no, wait a minute, guys. Take a deep breath and just cool it. Let's not panic here. Panicking never solves anything and usually only leads to wasted time and effort doing totally dumb things that don't make any difference. We're all reasonably intelligent people" she said looking around her "...er ...well... beings... and we can work this out. We've survived lots of crazy, dangerous situations before and we've triumphed over most of them. We can do it again, so just breathe deep and then let's make things happen. Now's the time to make the magick, guys."

Estelle gulped once and swallowed back her tears. Mary took a deep breath and dropped her librarian's finger. Sam shook his head once and sneezed, as if coming out of some kind of a fugue. A slight grin crept back on to his furry face.

"...and that is why they pay you the big bucks." he grinned at her "So, what exactly have you got in mind for us, oh fearless leader?"

Morgan blinked back at him. All she'd had in mind at the moment was to keep everyone from either blowing up or melting down, both behaviors that rarely yield anything useful and take time to recover from. They didn't have the time for histrionics now. The idea that she was now the one with the plan was new to her, and a lot of extra pressure, pressure she wasn't sure if she was ready for yet.

Usually in these adventures, her job was simply to stay alive, to run like mad, to not get caught, to follow the leader at any particular moment, and to learn more about the lands that lie between and beings that lived there, in the process of not dying. She wasn't sure if she was actually ready to be in charge yet, even if it was only this much.

"well..." she began slowly and hesitantly, carefully feeling her way through this "being the one in charge with the plan" thing "...let's start out by seeing if we can separate facts from story at all, and, within that, if we can separate the facts that are inevitable from the ones that the trooping fae may have learned from and therefore have changed. What do we know from our own knowledge versus what do we know from stories that may or may not still totally apply?"

Three sets of eyes focused on her very intently, expectantly waiting for any pearls of wisdom she was going to come out with and any brilliant plan she was about to let them in on. She had no plan, and as for pearls, of wisdom or otherwise, she hadn't even run across an oyster to irritate yet.

She wasn't used to this kind of rapt attention from her fellows. It was kind of disconcerting, actually. She'd never thought about how intimidating it must be to be a leader of an epic adventuring party, but, now that she was experiencing it for herself, she had a lot more sympathy for those stoic barbarian heroes and epic strategists.

"Let's try starting with what we already know about

the sidhe in general." said Morgan, tapdancing quickly.

"OK" said Sam thoughtfully. "And let's also note as we go along, what things we know for certain from our own experience versus what things we've only heard about. Let's consider the sources we've heard things from and whether that makes it more likely that these things have changed."

"Let's start with the fact that the sidhe are not human," said Morgan "that they're members of a magickal race of beings."

"But really magickal beings, they are not" said Estelle, carefully "as much as they are a race that magickal abilities has. Intrinsically magickal they are not. And not every one of them magickal abilities possesses, just as only certain human beings can magick do."

Morgan nodded. It was a legitimate distinction and one that might help them. "So you're saying that not every sidhe can do magick." she said thoughtfully. "and we might be able to use that."

"Yah." said Estelle "Able to immobilize us vith a vave of her hand the elven queen might be, but not every sidhe you meet vill that be able to do."

"One type of sidhe magick that we definitely know about," said Sam "is the so- called elven glamour. There are so many stories about the sidhe through history and our own experiences of their ability to make a person look like someone else or make a thing look different from its actual appearance. I think we can accept as fact that the illusion of an elven glamour is one of the challenges that we'll probably face."

"And speaking of enchantments" said Morgan "what exactly was that funky magickal thing that the Queen did that dropped us dead in our tracks during the rescue? The elven queen waved one hand and suddenly I dropped like a stone (into a nasty pricker bush, I might add). I couldn't move a muscle except for simple autonomic functions like breathing and blinking. That put a real crimp into trying to do anything including picking out any prickers digging their way into my skin."

"I've not seen that specific power before this," said Sam "but, for want of a better term, let's file it under the general category of "elven magick".

"and I don't want to hear any comments about making cookies in a hollow tree" he added in an irritable manner.

"Well, whatever you call it, we're gonna have to figure out something to deal with it." said Morgan "If the queen of the trooping sidhe can just wave her pretty little hand and drop us in our tracks, I don't think a second rescue will go much better than the first one."

They both turned and looked at Estelle then.

"Well?" said Sam

"Vell? Vell vhat?" the swan maiden said.

"Well, you're the shaman in this group and that means that you're the one in charge of all of the magick- y type stuff." said Sam "Got any nifty shamanic swan tricks to block an energetic straight jacket?"

"Vell, anything about that kind of thing I do not know." she protested emphatically. "Differently than this trooping fae kind of stuff, shamanic magick works. How ve can block it I really do not any idea have."

Mary blinked. "Oh wait. Wait just a minute" she said suddenly. "I just might have something that can help with

144

that. Let me see if I can find it again."

The librarian swept briskly out of the back carrels in a hurry, headed down towards the front desk. She moved with dispatch. She was now a woman on a mission.

They all looked after her. "Vhat that vas all about I vonder." said Estelle

"I don't really know" said Morgan, thoughtfully "but, given past experiences with her, I'm sure she'll come back with something wonderful and important. She's come through for us before."

"er... you know that a spirit she is, right?" said Estelle hesitantly. "like not a living, breathing human type being librarian, yes?"

"Well, nobody's perfect" said Sam "and yes we know that but thanks for the heads up."

"And leaving the question of elven magick for just a moment," he continued with a verbal flourish "the sidhe aren't human beings, but they're like humans in that they vary widely in intelligence and skills. We may be able to deceive or trick some of them. We've done it before."

"Also they're often beings of impulse. They take what they want. They do what seems to them worth doing. They can be distractable. We may be able to redirect them if we get them interested in something other than us."

"Despite being free ranging and fancy free like that," continued Sam 'the sidhe also seem to have rules that they follow, even must follow even if they don't want to. Part of the problem with that is that different groups also have different rules and we don't know what this group's rules are."

"This whole "grab hold of the guy and hang on no

matter what and you will win him back" thing seems to be pretty consistent rule over different groups of trooping sidhe and may be one of the rules for this group as well. It's been included in story after story and song after song, which is one possible proof that it still holds sway here, and you'll notice that, even though the queen said that they had learned a lot over many years of doing this, they haven't stopped riding, and, from what she said, he was there somewhere. They just used an elven glamour to disguise someone or something else as the expected knight. That implies that that's a rule that they must follow and are trying to work around. We can work with that to win Claud and Ariella free if we can find them."

"In keeping with these rules, the sidhe take their word very seriously and don't give it lightly. A promise or commitment from a sidhe is binding, so if you can get them to make one, they're bound by it- but they're also very tricky and will do their best to keep their word and still screw you over. As they're bound by contracts, promises and commitments, they're also very bad people to bargain with. Be careful about what you commit to, or even say around them," said the golden cat "for they'll hold you to it with a vengeance."

"They're vulnerable to certain things like cold iron" said Morgan thoughtfully. "They can't abide it. They can't touch it. It burns them."

"But remember how much it hurts varies greatly from sidhe to sidhe." responded Sam. "It can be deadly for one type of sidhe and a minor irritation for another. You may not be able to predict how much protection that cold iron will give you or how much damage it will do. Too much or too little can be equally bad. Too little means that the unseelie sidhe you hoped to immobilize with it gets up and keeps coming, and too much means the elven adversary you hoped to immobilize may up and die, leaving you open to a blood feud from his family and friends."

"And, believe me, you don't want to be on the receiving end of a blood feud with a troop of the fae." he added.

"And last," said the cat "the sidhe are loosely divided into two groups, the seelie and the unseelie. Strictly speaking, it's actually less two separate groups and more like a sliding scale of relatively friendly, comparatively benign or actively malevolent. Where any particular sidhe falls on that scale may depend upon his mood, what's best for him at the moment and what the weather's like, amongst other things."

"The unseelie sidhe are actively hostile and malevolent to humans, to other beings and to each other. Very dangerous, and if you run into one, smile, be polite and get away as quickly and cleanly as you possibly can."

"The seelie sidhe, on the other hand, are widely held by most folks to be far more favorable to humans and other beings. This may be the case or it just may be that they maim you by accident instead of actively trying to do so. They're also very dangerous but possibly more helpful to people like us, so use your own best judgment on a case by case basis"

Astonished, Morgan gaped widely at the golden cat "Wait a minute there, Sam" she said "some of our good friends are either partly or completely seelie sidhe, and they've helped us many times!"

"That's true," the golden cat solemnly nodded "but please don't forget that, even though they may really like you and may even be willing to help you out on occasion, they're still very dangerous. Indeed, on more than one occasion, the fact that they're very dangerous is the reason why they've been able to help you."

He watched her face very carefully as the thought sank in and she grew pale.

"Never forget that the land of faerie is neither a tame nor safe space" he said softly to her "It's certainly wild, yes, beautiful and wondrous, but above all, extremely hazardous. If you keep that in mind, you'll do all right."

"So dangerous to varying degrees the sidhe all are, but in their own oddly sidhe vay, kind some may also be." said Estelle thoughtfully. "A very good thing to be knowing that is. Vat do we actually know about the kind of the sidhe that the trooping bit do?"

"Well, it seems that they can be either seelie or unseelie, although they seem more likely to be unseelie sidhe," said Sam thoughtfully. "And they tend to ride at night along an established path way at specific times of the month."

"Together in a large group they ride," said Estelle "vith elven horses that faster them make and fierce hounds and keen hawks that their enemies can detect and also, if need be, them down hunt. All these things more dangerous them making."

"What we've learned from dowsing." said Morgan "is that the path is not only a standard path, but also, unlike most of the fae, their path winds back and forth between the lands that lie between and the lands of man without use of mobile gates and time windows. They do troop and do ride at specific times, but the action of trooping seems to make them free to pass between worlds."

"Their prisoners they take vith them vhen they troop." said Estelle. "On display, they them put. Their prisoners they show off. That they are proud, and possibly a little vain, that means– and a useful thing that may be to know."

"…and all the traditional tales say that the plucky girl who seizes her love as he rides by and holds on to him while he's turned from fearsome form to fearsome form to fearsome form can win him back from the trooping fae and take him home again." said Sam. "That's supported both by the literature and by the fact that these unseelie sidhe seem to have "learned" from this by substituting one of their own for the obvious target."

"Oh my…." said Morgan, with a funny little catch in her voice. The other two turned and looked at her.

She looked back at them with wide eyes, one finger marking a specific place in a book.

"…and evidently, they seem to need to pay a "teind to hell" every seven years." Morgan said with a flat tone in her voice.

Sam flinched and choked.

"A teind to hell? Vat that is?" said Estelle cautiously.

"I'm not sure if this is actually talking about Hell literally," Morgan said in a dispirited way "but there's evidently some kind of great power, probably evil, that requires from the trooping fairies a sacrifice to it of some kind of a sentient being on a regular basis."

"….a sacrifice? Vat kind of sacrifice?…" said Estelle

innocently. And then understanding came slowly into her eyes and her breath began to quicken. "but… vhy?"

"The old stories don't say why," Morgan stumbled on wards "but they do say that the sacrifice, the "teind" or tithe is most frequently someone they have captured."

"…but… that… that would mean that Ariella…" stuttered Estelle.

Sam looked somberly at both of them "That'd mean the trooping fae have an even more important reason to hang on to Claud, and now Ariella, than we realized at first." the golden cat said quietly. "We can guess this infernal power is powerful, or else such perilous beings as the trooping fae would not feel the obligation to turn someone over to it. If they don't have an outsider to pay their debts with, they'll have to turn over one of their own. This means that they have a strong incentive to keep prisoners beyond sheer amusement value and it'll be even harder to regain our people."

"…but …but…" stuttered Estelle, tears brimming once more in her eyes.

Sam leapt gracefully down from the carrel that he had been sitting in and crossed over to Estelle. "We'll get them back, Estelle" he said softly but firmly, placing a calming palm on her knee. "This just means the fae will be more motivated to keep them, so we're going to have to be even cleverer than they are. Hey, we're the heroes, so that should be a total tuna fish salad sandwich for us."

Estelle looked down at him and then smiled a bit tentatively, still teary eyed "Right that does not seem to be. Like a piece of cake I think you must mean, no?" she said.

"Nope. Not at all" the golden cat smiled up at her.

"I'm not that much for cake, but I can make a tuna fish salad sandwich disappear like nobody's business. I'm wishing this rescue to be as quick and easy for all of us as tuna is for me."

Sam and Estelle stood there for a moment gazing deeply into each other's eyes with Morgan looking on, all three of them taking comfort in this quiet point of calm before they had to go out into the storm again.

There was a moment of companionable silence between the three of them- a moment where their energies fused together and they were, for one moment, at one.

And then they heard the sound of footsteps hurrying towards them, and Mary swept back into the section of carrels they were hiding in….

Chapter 31
From Claud's View

She was so close. She was so very close to him. He could almost touch the swan princess from where he stood as she came leaping up from out of the gully, but the spells that bound him round made him unable to call out her name.

Instead, he did everything that he could to attract her attention to him and to protect her from the redcap that they had riding disguised in the position a captured knight would ride in according to all of the traditional tales.

She had fire and courage. He had to admit that. She moved quickly, efficiently, vigorously and effectively, and was actually upon and amongst the trooping sidhe before any of them realized she was there.

He tried his best to get between her and the redcap. The redcap was thoroughly disguised by the glamour upon him and the armor worn as part of its' disguise. He knew that if it took her in its grasp, terrible things would happen.

As indeed they did.

He failed, in part, because the swan princess was so determined to achieve her task that she got beyond him as well before he realized she was there. The best he could do was try to compensate for the time he had lost, and his efforts were too little, too late.

The swan princess vaulted swiftly through the air, hitting the knight riding closest to the town, as all of the traditional tales said a prisoner would be, and knocking him off the horse. She lay on the ground, staring up at the queen with her arms wrapped tightly around the knight she had claimed.

She smiled triumphantly up at the queen. And the queen of air and darkness smiled a horrid smile back down at her.

The queen gestured once. Just once. And then the glamor on the red cap melted away and his face was revealed.

The swan princess had stared at what had been revealed, afraid but resolute, clearly thinking that this was, this must be, one of the challenges she had to face to reclaim the captive. She held on firmly, not realizing this was not an illusion created in the moment, but rather one just stripped away.

This lasted only until the red cap pressed his rubbery lips to her shoulder and bit down hard, tearing away a chunk of her flesh and then grinning evilly at her.

The swan princess screamed out loud but still held onto the redcap, confused whether this was an elven challenge she needed to overcome or not. Blood flowed from her shoulder in torrents and the redcap chortled and bent to bite her once again, savoring her like a lovely swan steak. The other sidhe that ringed the pair round laughed as well, taking pleasure in her confusion and pain.

Claud dropped his head and wept. There was nothing he could do that would not do as much damage to her as to her oppressor.

The swan princess, growing faint from shock and blood loss, gradually loosened her grip on her captive. She was not as entertaining to the courtiers as she was initially and they remounted their horses and formed up once more. Freed from the grip of the swan princess, the redcap stood. He mounted a new steed, pulling her barely conscious form up onto his horse with him

The Queen called to her court that it was time to ride on,

And the trooping fairies continued their ride- with one new rider added to their ranks.

Chapter 32
At the Library

Mary came bustling back, carrying a cardboard box in her hands. Walking briskly over to one of the carrels, she rested the corner of the box on one shelf and pushed a pile of books to one side, clearing more space so there was enough room for the whole box.

She opened it and reached in, rummaging vigorously. "Now where are they?" she muttered to herself. "Where'd I put them, anyway?"

Talking under her breath, Mary continued to look through the box. Several minutes went by before she finally found what she was looking for. "There they are at last!" she said, pulling a manila envelope with colorful flowers with smiley faces drawn on it out of the box.

Morgan, Estelle and Sam all stared at her beaming face and waited a moment for an explanation.

"There what are at last?" said Sam after a moment, when no explanation was forthcoming.

Mary's eyes widened in surprise. "Oops!" she said "I was so happy to be able to find these in lost and found that I forgot you didn't even know what I went looking for."

She opened the manila envelope and reached deeply into it, pulling out a mass of small items. They were tangled together thoroughly, and at first Morgan couldn't visually sort out what the librarian was holding.

Mary gently shook her hand three times. The tangle fell apart, and delicate necklaces dangled below her hand

They were clearly home-made, fashioned with love and care. Each was made of two tiny twigs, crossing each other and carefully tied together with red thread. Each one hung from a long loop of cord also made of braided red thread.

They seemed simple enough, but Morgan had learned the hard way that, in the world of the lands that lie between, things weren't always what they seemed. These looked like simple necklaces, but Mary's gifts were often more than they first appeared.

Closing her one eye, Morgan looked through the eye that let her see magick and past glamours at the delicate necklaces that Mary held dangling from her hand. She saw a light shining all around them, a soft and twinkling rosy red aura that filled the air around the trinkets.

Mary had a triumphant look on her face as she held out the amulets and observed the three of them.

"Rowan and red thread." whispered Sam under his breath. "Rowan and red thread. Now why didn't I think of that?"

Mary twinkled at him. "Rowan and red thread, indeed." she said, happy in a job well done.

"Er…" said Morgan "you know that some of us are enchantment challenged. I can tell that something pretty good is going on here but I'm darned if I know what. Some subtext here, please? What exactly is rowan and red thread, and why's it a good thing in our current situation?"

Estelle smiled at her. "Of this one, at least I know. Rowan and red thread," she said "a traditional protection against negative energy and the negative influences of all enchanted creatures it is. Against evil magick and the Evil Eye, and from being carried off to Faerie against one's will it can also you protect."

"Traditional rowan and red thread charms" said Sam, going into lecture mode "were made either in the form of two rowan twigs formed into crosses and tied together with red thread or else twigs stripped of bark with notches marked into them; and they needed to be remade and recharged regularly. They were hung by doorways, tied to the tails of valuable animals such as cattle, and carried in the pocket or worn for protection."

"And these are absolutely perfect for our situation" he said with delight, abandoning his professorial manner as quickly as he had assumed it. "I don't know why I didn't think of this before." He nuzzled at the dangling necklaces, playfully batting at one.

"Possibly because it's just simple folk magick." said Mary, lifting them slightly above his paws. "They're more like a judo throw as opposed to a punch in the nose. These charms won't make you invulnerable to elven magick, or to a direct physical assault like a sword or elf shot, but they'll give you some resistance to elven charms, spells and other malign influences. That may be just the edge you need to come out on top and to get your friends back from the trooping sidhe before they meet some far grimmer fate."

"So, where did they come from?" asked Morgan, intrigued by the delicate little charms.

Mary looked a tad abashed. "Well," she said "that's the problem. We're not quite sure about that."

"About a week back," said Mary "we had an extra busy week here at the library. A lot of books going out and coming back, and sometimes it took longer to get all of the books back on the shelves. The human librarians usually deal with reshelving but I noticed things were piling up and decided to help out. I can't stand it when books are lingering behind the desk and not getting out there where people can enjoy them again."

"I waited until the library shut down and everyone had gone," said Mary "I loaded up a library cart and began to make the rounds, putting books back as I went. I knew there were so many books waiting to go back on the shelves that the day librarians wouldn't notice that a cart or two had gotten back on their own, as long as I chose an assortment of books."

"I was working my way around the various sections of the library and at last got to the folklore and magick section, the same one you've pulled all of these books from." said Mary "I shelved one book and another; but when I went to shelve a third book on a high shelf, I could see the gap it belonged in, but when I tried to push it in, it just wouldn't go."

"I tried once, twice and even a third time, but the book just wouldn't slide into place," said Mary. "It felt like there was something already there on the back of the shelf, on the part I couldn't see."

"It wouldn't be the first time a book fell off the shelf," said Mary "and was cross wards on the back of it, blocking other books from their places; so I stopped, got a rolling stool and climbed up to see what was interfering with my shelving."

"Climbing up, I stood on my toes to see to the back of the shelf. In the shadows at the back, I caught a glimpse of something other than a book." said Mary "Reaching carefully, I found myself holding this envelope."

"I climbed down and looked at it for a moment," said

Mary "When you're talking about something carefully hidden on the back of a top shelf in an obscure corner of the library, it could be anything from interesting to malign, from a bomb to drugs to someone's secret love letters. While, as a spirit, there's not a lot that could harm me, I didn't want to do any damage to the library itself or the people and the books in the process."

"I stopped then." said Mary "I gave it some thought. Then I took precautions. I carefully carried the envelope downstairs to the underground parking garage. It was the middle of the night, so there weren't any people there, and not many vehicles - only the book mobile and I stayed on the far side of a column from that. I carefully laid the envelope down on an open section of asphalt and went back to the library to get tools to work with. I was able to use a long-handled ruler and a telescoping pointer to hold the envelope down from a distance, tease the flap open and coax the contents out into the open where I could see what they were."

"Once I could tell I wasn't going to unleash anything like Ebola or cyanide or a tiny little fiendish explosive device," Mary said "I tentatively examined the envelope contents more closely. What I found in the envelope was a good-sized handful of these rowan and red thread necklaces and a note."

By now, all three adventurers were intrigued. "What was in the note, Mary?" asked Sam curiously

"That was the odd part" said Mary hesitantly. "It was a piece of parchment, not old or antique, but certainly distinctive. It had words written in an almost calligraphic hand; and it said *"There will be a need for shielding and protection. Take these tokens, freely given and freely received, and use them wisely to help to address a great injustice. "*

"And the note was not signed."

"Whoa. The whole thing sounds odd to me." said Sam.

"Oh, not so odd as you might think" said Mary smiling widely. "You'd be really surprised if you knew about the things that just show up in a library, especially one as energetically active as this one."

"They… just… showed… up." said Morgan thoughtfully. "We have a magickal crisis and something that's an answer to one of our urgent needs, one that could make or break our situation, just happens to show up."

"Does that seem overly convenient to anybody besides me? Does anyone else here think there might be some strings attached to these convenient little amulets?"

"Any strings attached?" said Estelle, puzzled. "Vell of course, some strings attached there are. The strings, they are the part that around our necks go, no?"

Morgan gaped at her. She hadn't thought about it, but she could understand how it could sound that way to someone who had swan as their primary language, and German as their second.

"No, I'm sorry, Estelle. That's not what I meant." she said carefully. "I meant that, when you have a big problem and someone presents you with a perfect solution, that person may have ulterior motives that may not be in your best interests. Didn't your mother ever teach you to not take candy from strangers?"

"Actually, teach me my mother did candy from strangers to take," said Estelle "and horses, and jewelry, and big bags of gold and silver coins, and thick ham sandwiches, and anything else that my fancy struck; and if they tried to stop me, to them hit. Remember, a society of varriors making our living from raiding and looting other people ve are, and most of them happen strangers to be."

"In a more civilized manner, I am trying to behave. A big disappointment to mein mother I am." she said, smoothing her hair back in an exaggerated manner. "But, besides that, vhat I am hearing from vhat you are saying is that you are thinking that these amulets a trap of some sort might be?"

"Oh, not a trap created by Mary" said Morgan quickly, as the librarian hearth spirit began to frown at her "but rather a trap created by someone else and left in our path in the hopes that we might trigger it and do ourselves some harm. We really don't know where these came from, and they do seem very convenient. It's more than a bit worrisome."

"Then good it is you have a shaman vith you who knows vays of on such things checking, eh?" the swan shaman said serenely. "Much about the magic of the fae I may not know, but a lot about traps I do."

Unselfconsciously, Estelle turned to Mary and held out her right hand to her with a quiet assurance. Mary looked at her carefully and then gently dropped the red thread and rowan amulets into her hand.

Estelle held the red thread and rowan amulets gingerly. She looked into the hand that held them and gently poked them with the index finger of her other hand, turning them side to side so she could examine them more carefully. After a minute or so, she pursed her lips and began to hum

163

quietly to herself.

Quietly, yes, but the quiet hum quickly seemed to swell to fill the great halls of the library, rebounding off the concrete and steel and glass until Morgan's head began to throb in time with it. You'd think that all of the books would have some kind of muffling effect, but the sound of the humming continued to swell, despite all of the sound insulation available to them.

"That's not natural." Morgan thought, and then she thought again and closed her one eye so that only her seeing eye was looking at Estelle and what she was doing with the amulets.

Estelle continued to hum and poke, poke and hum, but as Morgan looked with her with the eye with magickal sight, she could see something else. Before, when she'd looked at the amulets, they'd shone with a faint but noticeable soft red glow for those with the sight to see beyond illusions. Now, as Estelle hummed and poked, poked and hummed, the rose red glow around the red thread and rowan amulets became brighter, more solid and also grew in size until it shone into the area, completely surrounding the contemplative swan shaman. It shone out, surrounding her outside of her personal aura or energy shield, like a protective outer layer.

Morgan looked at Sam, and opened her mouth to say something about this to him

At that moment, Estelle stopped humming and then looked up at them, her eyes clearing and focusing. "Know I do not exactly who these made." she said thoughtfully. "No specific maker's mark on them there is. but definitely no harm in them there is; and a great deal of good there is. I

164

would say that safely these amulets we can use, and that they may help us safe to stay and our friends to save."

"That's good enough for me." said Sam "I'll take all of the help that I can get. What exactly can they do for us, Estelle?"

Estelle looked down at the amulets still nestled in her right hand. Her eyes got dreamy for a moment. It was as if she were looking at something a long way off.

After a moment, her eyes came into focus again.

"Vell, super powers they vill not us give" she said "Against the magick of the sidhe, especially the magick of the Queen, invulnerable they vill not us make but more resistant to elven magick help us to be they vill. There may some illusions be ve shall not through see, and, to a lesser extent, to other kinds of elven magick, ve may still partly vulnerable be."

"But protect us enough they may so that for the rescue ve can keep on moving rather than like stones drop vhenever the Queen her cute little elven hand at us she vaves."

"And frankly, right now, to me like a pretty good deal that sounds."

A big grin spread across Sam's beautiful furry face. "You know, I would really enjoy having even that much control on the magickal front." he said gleefully.

"And me as well." said Estelle "Vatching the Queen wave her cute little elven hand at us I could really enjoy, if I could right in her eye look, a raspberry in her face blow, and our friends back grab. Foolish it may be, but, for once, a little look of confusion or even concern on her too perfect, too beautiful elven face I would like to see, nein?"

Sam grinned even wider at the thought. "So how do these amulets work, Estelle?" he said "Is there anything special we have to do, or know?"

"Easy peasy to make them for us vork it is." Estelle said "Around our necks or on our persons ve have only to them vear. No magickal vords or mystic powers required are. You carry them, they vork."

"That's convenient" said Sam "because my guess is we'll be busy with lots of other things to do during this rescue, and anything that doesn't require extra knowledge or skills is a good thing."

Estelle shook the bundle of red thread and rowan amulets gently and detached one from the bundle in her hand. "Just like this, you vill it vear." she said, leaning forwards and placing the necklace around the golden cat's soft and fuzzy neck, adjusting a slider bead so it hung at the right level for Sam to be able to move freely without tangling his paws.

Sam looked down at the amulet and lifted up one paw to gently brush the cross where it hung at his throat. "Not too shabby." he said "I don't usually wear jewelry but I could make an exception in this case."

Morgan closed one eye and looked with her seeing eye. Sam's aura was still present and looked healthy but was now surrounded by an additional soft red border on the outside. Estelle's natural aura was also surrounded by the red thread and rowan energy. It seemed the amulets did provide some additional energy or protection without interfering with the energy field of the person wearing it, whether you wore or carried it

Estelle turned to her then. She shook out another

amulet and placed it gently around Morgan's neck. Morgan felt a slight tingling, but didn't otherwise feel different, but, when she looked at her own energy, she could see the red thread and rowan layer laid over the outside of her own field.

Estelle turned to Mary and offered her the remaining amulets.

Mary looked thoughtful. "How many people are you trying to rescue?" she asked.

"As far as we know, two" said Morgan "but it's the lands of enchantment, so who can really say?"

"Then, you should probably have enough amulets to provide protection from elven magick for those people too" said Mary "with maybe a spare as well. Just in case."

Mary took the necklaces. She teased three of them out of the bunch of jewelry and handed them to Morgan, holding on to the rest. "There you go" Mary said. "and hopefully those will give you the edge you need."

"Thanks, Mary" said Morgan "that takes care of one challenge. And when it comes to the question of elven glamours, I may have a remedy for that problem at least. I used the ointment of seeing you gave me the last time we visited in only one eye, and I still have the ability to see through glamours. I'm hoping to use that to see through any illusions the fae cast so we can rescue Claud and Ariella."

Mary nodded. "That seems sound," she said "as long as you're the first one up since you'll be spotting targets and traps."

"Right" said Morgan "problems with that are part of why we failed the first time."

"But next time, that's going to be different." said Sam. "If we co-ordinate better, Morgan will get the chance to look before we leap- or at least while we leap.

"A good thing, I think that vould be." said Estelle. "If where the traps are hidden ve can know, maybe avoid them ve can. If sooner our folks we find, a better chance of getting avay vith them before too much harm the sidhe can do to us ve have."

"Well, we've got a plan for dealing with glamours," said Sam "and we have a plan to keep the queen from stopping us dead, but I can't help thinking that there's more we need to do to prepare for tonight."

"You know, it sounds like it might be a good idea for you to contact your friends at the court of the Seelie sidhe next see if you can get any help from them or at least additional advice." said Mary as she tucked the remaining amulets away.

"You may be right." said Sam thoughtfully "but we'll first have to see where and when the doors to the lands that lie between will open next. Since the doors aren't stable and aren't always in one place, we'll have to catch the magickal window when they open in this plane if we're going to cross over to the enchanted lands and visit the court for any aid and information. Our time's tight now, and getting tighter all the time. We'd need to hit the time window to cross over, but we'll also need to catch the next window to be back in time to catch the trooping fairies before they make their third and final ride"

"The other possibility, of course," he said "is that some of the more knowledgeable and helpful folks from the seelie court, ones that already owe us, might possibly be over on this side of the veil, and more accessible to us. There's just an outside chance that someone who could help us and might be willing to do so might be on this side of the great divide."

"Let's see, shall we?" said Morgan and reached into the interior pocket of her purse. Withdrawing her hand from the purse, she slowly released the weight end of her pendulum, letting it swing freely from its cord.

Bending over the flat surface of the carrel, she went to work looking for folks who might help them.

Chapter 33
Back in the Oubliette

The sidhe lifted Claud's glamour, loaded him with chains again and dropped him twenty feet down the shaft of the oubliette into the standing water at the bottom.

"One more ride." one sneeringly called down to him. "One more night."

"And then you shall have a new master."

And the door overhead banged shut, plunging him into darkness alone with his thoughts.

Alone with his thoughts.

Claud had a thought. Once before, in solitude, damp and darkness, he had reached out with his thoughts in desperation- and he remembered an impression of contacting someone else's thoughts for a moment.

"Maybe that again I could do." Claud thought. "It is not like anything else I have to do. Let us again that try."

And, closing his eyes, calling on his will and focusing his thoughts, he reached out...

Chapter 34
<u>Contact Morgan</u>

As the pendulum swung, Morgan closed her eyes to avoid influencing the results and concentrated on getting the information that could help them succeed in the rescue.

Suddenly she found herself looking into familiar blue eyes.

"It's Claud!" she thought.

She focused her will, set an intention to make contact and reached out as hard as she could.

"Claud, it's Morgan" she thought. "We're going to try to rescue you, but we need all the information that you can give us to help us succeed."

The blue eyes widened.

Chapter 35
Contact Claud

Claud jumped as he found himself looking into grey eyes he recognized.

"Claud, it's Morgan." he heard in his head. "We're going to try to rescue you, but we need all the information you can give us to help us succeed."

He had made contact. He had made contact!

But who knew how well that contact would work or how long it would last?

He narrowed his eyes and focused his thoughts, trying to make the most of the unexpected link. He focused on the image of a white horse. "Last night." he thought desperately "One more night only, the fae ride…"

And then the link shattered.

Chapter 36-
Dowsing for Information

And then the link shattered.

Morgan shook. She'd had a link but she'd lost it again, and losing that contact might mean losing Claud and Ariella forever.

She wasn't ready to accept that.

She looked down at the pendulum, as it gently swung up and down below her hand. She closed her eyes, taking a deep breath and then letting it slowly out again. She repeated the breath twice more to calm and center herself and bring herself into harmony with the pendulum and the energy surrounding it.

She opened her eyes once she was ready to start.

"Stop, please." she said, and the pendulum stopped swinging immediately.

"Thank you. Show me yes, please." said Morgan, and the pendulum immediately began to swing up and down once more.

"Show me no, please." she said, and the pendulum wobbled around for a bit and then changed its direction from up and down to side to side.

"Stop, please." she said at last, and the pendulum gradually came to a stop.

She was ready now. She was ready to dowse.

Her companions came over to watch her work, Estelle standing on her right side, and Mary hovering on her left. Sam leaped gracefully up onto the back of the carrel, balancing gracefully on an impossibly small surface by clever use of toes and tail and sheer presence besides.

He peered down at her in an interested fashion. He'd often seen her use a pendulum before, but in life there was always something new to be observed, learned or just plain adapted, and Sam was a very curious cat indeed.

"What do you want me to start with?" she asked the onlookers "Shall we ask first about whether the path and the timing the trooping fairies shall take will be the same as last night, or shall we ask about when and where the gates open to the lands that lie between?"

"Let's start with the riding of the sidhe." said Sam "We need that knowledge first, and then we can see how gating across the worlds fits into that."

"Makes sense." said Morgan, and started asking her pendulum questions about where, when and how often the troop of unseelie sidhe would ride again.

As always, it took a while to get information out of the pendulum. The pendulum was consistently accurate within the limitations of free will, but, since it could only answer questions with either a yes or a no, any complex information had to be obtained through a series of elimination questions.

Was this right? No. Then how about this? And so forth. Half the trick with a pendulum lay in learning how to ask good questions that worked with this method of divination.

On the plus side, they'd previously dowsed for the path that the trooping fairies would ride, so they were able to save a lot of time by asking "Is this the same as last night?". On the negative side, there were still a lot of things yet to be checked, at the maddening snail's pace of yes and no.

And time was running out for them all.

"The traditional tales say the fae troop for three nights. Is that true?" Morgan asked her pendulum.

The answer came back as yes.

"And which night of three was last night? Three?" asked Morgan, her heart in her mouth because that would mean that their chance to save their fellows would have come and gone for this month.

No.

"What about night two then?" she went on.

Yes. Which meant that their last chance this month to regain Claud and Ariella would be tonight. Tonight or not at all this month.

"And how soon is the teind to hell? Within this year?" she asked the pendulum.

"Yes" said the pendulum.

"Within six months?" she went on.

"Yes" said the pendulum

"Within three months?" she went on, her heart sinking.

"Yes."

"Within this month?" she went on.

"Yes."

Which meant that tonight was their last chance ever to regain Claud and Ariella before they were sacrificed to some infernal power.

Her three companions didn't seem to have realized what the pendulum had said yet and what that meant for them all.

"Guys," Morgan said, trying to restrain panic in her voice "The teind to hell happens this month. Tonight is the

179

last fairie rhade before the prisoners are sacrificed."

Slowly, the color drained out of Estelle's face until she was dead white. "The very last night tonight is?" she whispered. "Vhat will ve do? Not enough time to figure it all out there is. Not enough time them to save."

There was a long pause.

Then Sam climbed out along the edge of the carrel and put a soft paw on her face. "We'll pull it out." he said "We'll save them, because that's what heroes do; and evidently we are once again in the position of unlikely heroes triumphing over impossible odds."

"Morgan" he went on, still cradling Estelle's stricken face "Keep working on it. What good news do you bring us?"

Morgan's pendulum was already swinging once again. "Bad news to start with." she muttered. "The gates between the lands of man and the lands that lie between will open before the next elven rhade, but they will only open once before we need to be in position, so there's not enough time for us to nip across for advice or help, and get back in time to meet the trooping fae. Those gates open again two hours later, but that means we'll miss the rhade and miss saving our friends as well."

"On a varrior training veekend on the other side of de mountains, mein flock is now. No way to bring them in in time for backup der is." Estelle snuffled. "Ariella and I had in town stayed because the var games that they had planned ve vas not really interested in."

"And both the palmist and tarot reader are way down south working at a renaissance faire so they're only good for giving us advice by phone." added Sam. "It looks like everyone we might possibly get some help from, other than Mary, is out of touch or out of reach right now. That's bad news indeed."

"The news is not completely bad." said Morgan, looking intently at her still swinging pendulum. "We definitely can't make it over to the lands that lie between and back in time, but it seems that there's one visitor from the seelie court over here on this side of the barrier. Believe it or not, the seelie elven king is currently visiting the lands of man, and, if my pendulum's accurate, he's taking tea and sandwiches in the tea shop where I first met him, not far from here."

Sam did a double take. "He's what?" he said loudly, triggering a shush from Mary. "The king of the seelie sidhe and of the lands that lie between is having tea in a tea shop in the lands of man? And not even an enchanted tea shop? You'd think that he had more important or more delicious things to do with himself, being the king of the lands that lie between."

Morgan shrugged "Go figure." she said "It's worth noting they do make very good sandwiches in that shop. Besides, I'd imagine that, if one was a king, there would probably be times when you'd want to get away for a while and do something with less pomp and circumstances."

"Be that as it may" said Sam urgently "Time's wasting. Let's go!"

Morgan dropped her pendulum in its pouch, and dropped it into its pocket in her purse. She held the main area of the purse open wide and Sam jumped gracefully into it for the ride out of the library. Estelle grabbed their other miscellaneous gear and all three moved as a unit towards the staircase.

Mary stayed behind them waving them on. "Good luck and good fortune." she cried out, and waved vigorously until the three were out of sight again.

Then she sighed and began to reshelve the books that they'd left in uneven stacks behind them.

Chapter 37
Meeting with the Seelie King

The bus pulled up in front of the Spot O' Tea, and Estelle and Morgan got off, Sam riding securely in Morgan's over-sized hand bag. The bell jingled as they entered and looked around.

"Deja view." thought Morgan. "I have seen this particular tea shop before."

The tea shop was tiny and crowded and full of tables filled with older women chattering together, women taking a short break from intense shopping, grandmothers out with their granddaughters in their very best dresses; and one extremely large figure completely overshadowing a table in the back.

The king of the seelie sidhe was taking his ease at a tea shop table, with a large chicken with pesto sandwich on rustic bread and an enormous double sized mug of tea. He was dressed as he had been when Morgan had first met him in his everyday working outfit of biker's leathers with an over-sized leather coat and a bandana on his head, and he showed every sign of enjoying his current busman's holiday.

He looked up and his eyes met Morgan's as she and Estelle edged their way between the other tightly packed tables towards the place where he was sitting. A quick look of confusion crossed his face briefly, to be replaced by a genial expression suitable for most occasions.

"Ladies" he said as they reached his table "May I invite you to take a seat and join me? The chicken with pesto sandwiches are particularly good today, but I can also recommend the chocolate mousse cake."

Morgan bent down to better gain the king's ear. "That would be lovely," she said quietly "but we find ourselves in a bit of a situation and we could use your help. We hate to trouble you but would it be possible for you to join us at one of the outside tables where we could speak more freely?"

The king sighed. "There is no rest for the busy," he said "but of course, it will, as always, be my pleasure, my lady."

He looked over to the service counter. "Peg!" he bellowed. Everybody jumped slightly. "I'm moving outside for a bit. Can you bring out three more of those chicken with pesto sandwiches and three more of the big mugs of green tea?"

"Four" said Morgan's handbag. "Four sandwiches."

"Make that four sandwiches." shouted the king, as he stood up. "Thank you, love."

The woman behind the counter grinned broadly and began to assemble his order as the king moved carefully towards the tea shop door, Morgan and Estelle in tow.

Chapter 38
Ariella

Ariella came gradually back to herself, held firmly in place on the back of the gelding in the implacable grip of the red cap. She kept her eyes partially shut, feigning semi-consciousness while trying to gather any information she could that could help her to escape.

"Vell, that one I surely a mistake made." she thought. "Though right I could have svorn I vas…"

She felt hot breath on her neck, and was glad she had her eyes mostly shut. That face she didn't want to see again, especially as close as it felt.

The swan people heal quickly and the bleeding from the bite on her shoulder was already slowing, although the bite still hurt with every rocking movement of the horse.

"Before the red cap a meal of me makes, I just hope that I can escape." she thought. "What comes next I wonder."

And then the faerie rhade reached its destination,

And she found out.

Chapter 39
Tea and Traditions

The waitress settled the tray on the café table in the nook outside of the tea shop and unloaded an assortment of sandwiches, big mugs of tea and other assorted tea shop goodness. She took the money the king handed to her, smiled at them once, and then went back into the tea shop to make other people happy.

The king took a big bite of his new sandwich and chased it with an epic draft of tea. Thus fortified, he took a deep breath and looked at them, his eyes twinkling.

"Well now, I am pretty sure that you ladies have not come here purely for the tea or for the sandwiches, good as both of them are, or even for the pleasure of my company; and I am also fairly sure that you would not choose to interrupt my day of leisure for no good reason at all. I am guessing that you have something important to bring to my attention. So, tell me, what is it, my ladies? I am in your debt, Morgan, and would gladly help you if I possibly can."

Morgan took a deep drink of her tea. There was so much to say and so little time it was hard to know where to start.

Sam had no such hesitations. "We have a crisis, your majesty." he said, pushing his head out of the purse. "We learned that one of the swan people is being held a prisoner by the queen of air and darkness and her trooping sidhe. We tried to rescue him and instead, Ariella, swan princess of the Mantel Fiedervolk, was also taken captive. We have until tonight to set them both free before the unseelie sidhe must pay a teind to hell and our friends are gone beyond our reach

187

for good and all."

"We've come to you, your majesty, for help and advice," said Sam "and I also would not mind one of those chicken sandwiches that I see sitting up there on the table."

The king picked up a plate with a chicken sandwich on it, and bent to place it on the ground in front of the cat. When he straightened, his face was serious.

"Then we have a bit of a problem here." said the king "I am sorry, but I am not sure how much I can help you."

"Wait just a minute here" said the cat, raising his head from an already half-finished sandwich "I thought that, after our first encounter with you, you were not only the king of the seelie sidhe, but also the ruler of all of the sidhe. What gives, your majesty?"

The king shook his head. "It is true that I am officially the ruler of all of the lands that lie between and all of the beings who live there;" said the king "but it is also true that the members of the unseelie sidhe and certain other groups like the trooping fae, will often play their own games and do not always follow the laws that I have set for my kingdom. Even more so, the trooping fairies tend to have their own little societies and their own customs and laws that may be very different than the laws that I have set. They may not follow my laws. I may not even know all of their customs and laws because each troop goes its own way."

"In addition, the balance between the different factors of the fae is always shaky." said the king. "There are some things that openly break my law, and there I may choose to act, but there are some things that are within their rights by law and tradition, and one of them is to take prisoners and to hold them as their own, and there my influence is more limited."

"Wait a minute" said Morgan "They have the right to capture people?"

The king shook his head. "They do indeed," he said "and have had that right back to the dawn of time. History is full of stories of this practice, and if I acted against it, much of the world of Faerie would rise in revolt."

"Even if I do not like that they do these things, if I take action against them when they are taking their rights according to law and tradition, I may give the unseelie world in general an excuse to declare open war between unseelie and seelie, so I must think about such actions carefully."

Morgan's mind locked up. She had hoped that the king could help them, but it seemed that, yet again, they were on their own.

"However, what I can do" said the king "is to tell you what I know about how these situations work. Now I would assume that you have already looked into the classic tales about trooping fae and how to win back a prisoner from them."

"We have…" said Morgan, trying hard not to look abandoned "but when we followed the classic tale, it didn't work and we just ended up losing Ariella."

"Well, let me give you more of the truth behind the tales" said the king "and let us see if that helps you."

"First, a glamor or illusion may be used by the fae at any time, so anything you can do to deal with that will help. Be aware that things are not necessarily what they seem to be."

Morgan nodded. They had lost Ariella because she tried to free the wrong target. The gel that would let Morgan see through glamours hopefully would keep that from happening again.

"A rescuer can be attacked physically or magickally by any and all of the unseelie sidhe before they grab hold of their target, and if you grab the wrong target, you have no protection from this." the king continued. "Once you have grabbed your target and gotten a good hold, no one can attack you, save only the queen. She can only attack using illusions to scare you or to make you believe that you're being hurt to make you let go; or transforming your target into something that may hurt you or be hard to hold onto."

"If the rescuer lets go, your target is once again a prisoner and the rescuer is fair game to be attacked by the entire troop."

"While the queen is trying to get you to let go, the prisoner may be transformed into a certain number of different forms before the target returns to its natural form. Tradition tends to say three forms, but that is not necessarily the case. Nobody actually knows how many forms it actually is (except possibly the queen.)"

"And finally," said the king "once your target returns to its natural form, you have won and can reclaim your person. The trials however are at that point over and you are both once again vulnerable to attack from any and all of the trooping fairies, including the queen. They may all be very angry at this point- so it is best to have an exit strategy." Morgan released a breath she hadn't realized she was holding. Put in context like this, she could see why they had failed and how they just might be able to change that.

They had a method of seeing through glamours and picking the correct target. They had a way to protect

190

themselves from attack and protect Claud and Ariella. They knew the facts on how this was supposed to work as opposed to just guessing based on traditional sources.

They just might be able to pull this off…

She looked up and into the sympathetic eyes of the seelie king. "Thanks." she said "That really does help."

"I wish that I could help you more." he said. "I can at least wish you well on your quest, and see if I can find any other way that I can help you all."

"Well, time's passing fast." said Sam. "We'd best get moving. Thank you, your majesty."

The king looked thoughtfully after them as they left the café. "I wonder…" he said. "Maybe there is a way to help them that will not make things worse."

.

Chapter 40
Try, Try Again

Once again, they were crouched down in the gully besides the track the trooping sidhe rode along. They'd chosen a position earlier along the path to try to avoid being predictable, and the slope was steeper than it had been on their previous rescue attempt.

"It's going to be even harder to charge up than the slope before." thought Morgan. "I hope that I can make it before they hear me coming."

She began small weight shifts and stretches to try to keep her legs from falling asleep while she waited. Estelle crouched patiently beside her.

"They're coming" whispered Sam, and Morgan's heart caught in her throat.

Once again, they could see a gleam of uncanny light and hear a distant jingle of harness and echo of voices like small silver bells approaching them in the distance around a bend in the causeway,

As before, the herald came first, blowing on his shining horn to clear the way for the court following. Grooms, hunters and lesser servants of the court came next, followed by falconers with birds on fist, resplendent in their ornate hoods and jesses

The lesser knights came next, each in his master's livery, riding in formation and prepared to defend the nobles. Their horses were deeply caparisoned and minced down the path.

The cluster of ladies followed thereafter, laughing and chattering to one another as they rode. Silk and satin shone in the enchanted light, but not as brightly as their flowing hair and shining faces as they rode in the elven train, flanked by elven knights. Silver bells jingled on their ankles and depended from the barding of their high stepping palfreys

A skillful minstrel in parti-colored clothing rode once more in close attendance on the ladies, lute in hand, singing and strumming bright and cheerful songs of love as he rode

Hounds and brachettes and retrievers of all shapes and sizes and colors ran back and forth along the length of the procession, whining eagerly, or stopping dead at a sharp command from an elven master, each dog perfect of his breed in looks, manner and comportment, and not a flaw amongst them. There were even a few dark hunds that ran loose amongst the rest of them, although other members of the pack tended to give them a wide margin of space when permitted by their masters or the huntsmen, who cracked their whips to call the pack to order.

And then, at long last, came the greater knights, each a sidhe champion in his own right. As before, their lances were held at ease and swords at the ready, prepared to defend their ruler if there was a threat.

Their Queen. In the heart of the elven train she rode, the Queen of Air and Darkness, beautiful and dark and dangerous, seated high upon an ebon steed. Skin as pale as moonlight and hair as red as fire, caught up in an elaborate braiding and studded with a fortune of pearls and precious gems. Eyes that promised love and danger and mysteries.

Morgan, Estelle and Sam crouched deeper into the gully, hoping they could hide themselves in the moment

The herald had passed and the falconers and grooms. The lesser knights passed, and the ladies and their minstrel.

"How can we do this?" thought Morgan. "We failed the last time and there are less of us now."

And then she had a moment of clarity. She listened to herself and what she'd been saying since this rescue began, and realized she'd been telling herself that she was going to fail. Her self-talk was programming her to give up and give in.

But what if she set an intention that they were going to succeed instead?

In her memory, she heard her teacher saying "If you watch what you tell yourself, whether out loud or in your head, and catch yourself when you tell yourself something negative, you can correct that by telling yourself something positive..."

She could do that.

"We're going to rescue Ariella and Claud. We're going to rescue Ariella and Claud. We're going to rescue Ariella and Claud." she silently repeated.

And suddenly she found herself racing up the hill, knowing, just knowing, that now was the time to act.

Tradition said that the captive knight would ride upon a white horse on the side of the procession closest to the town as a sign of honor. Morgan knew from their last experience that the trooping sidhe were not necessarily following those rules, but she could see a knight passing on a white horse up above and somehow, her intuition said that this was a sign

Morgan went leaping up the side of the gully and on to the path, Estelle at her side. The knight on the white horse had almost reached the point where Morgan stood, and it was the work of but a moment to reach him. The nervous white horse was prancing and rearing up on its hind legs. It shied away from her and fought against its rider's hands on the reins. Morgan ran straight at the massive horse and, reaching it, leapt up and on to its back, knocking its armored, helmeted rider off of the broad back of his ivory mount.

They both hit the ground hard, Morgan landing on top. The force of the impact knocked the wind out of her, making her dizzy, but still she held tightly to the figure clasped securely in her arms. The horse rose up on its hind legs in alarm and then dropped heavily down to the ground again, striking out at both of them with heavy hooves as they rolled beneath him in the shadows on the ground.

And lying there in the dirt with her arms around the knight, Morgan looked up at the white horse shying and rearing above them.

Into familiar bright blue eyes,

And she had another moment of intuition and clarity.

She looked through her seeing eye and confirmed what her intuition told her. She let go of the knight and lunged up to throw her arms around the horse's neck. The horse reared and pulled her to standing in the process.

The knight turned over and reached out for her.

Still clutching the horse's neck, she put one foot on the knight's chest and pushed hard, rolling him over the side and down the hill into the gully she had just rushed up out of.

There was the sound of multiple impacts as a heavy body rolled out of control down a steep slope, alternating with oofs, groans and other sounds of pain. The entire elven train froze, looked and listened to the thuds; and Morgan took advantage of the pause to get a better hold on the horse and look around.

She spotted the pale dog that had been running beside the horse, the one with violet eyes like Ariella's. She looked at it with her seeing eye, and confirmed her suspicions.

"Estelle!" she cried, still clinging to the horse. "There!"

Estelle seized onto the pale hound.

There was the sound of a final extra heavy thunk at the bottom of the gully; and then the fae all turned to stare hard at Morgan and Estelle

"Ooo boy!" said Estelle "In it now for sure ve are!"

The trooping fae made a circle around them, as they clutched their captives tighter. The queen of the troop rode slowly through her subjects until she was facing the interlopers. She smiled- the smile of someone who was enjoying something nasty.

"Thieves" the elf queen hissed "Come to steal our prisoners. How entertaining."

"So, ladies" she said in a low and deadly voice "you have come to challenge us. Very well. Just remember, you can only keep what you can hold."

The troop broke into unpleasant laughter and the queen gestured once.

A chime sounded, clear and piercing, echoing through the woods- and with the chime, Morgan felt the horse's body begin to twist and shift within her grasp. It changed shape and became shaggy and strong and howled as it struggled for its freedom.

The troop howled in unison with it in mockery.

Morgan could feel the snap of teeth biting at her head and neck, and claws striking at her body. She screwed her eyes shut, ducked her head into the shaggy chest to try to protect her face and eyes, and pressed her body against the broad shaggy chest to minimize the parts of her that were vulnerable. She could hear Estelle gasping and struggling and could only assume that she was also trying desperately to hold on to her charge.

"Hold on tight." she told herself. "Just hold on."

After an eternity, the chime rang again.

Morgan felt the broad, body in her grasp shift again and become longer and leaner. The limbs that gave her purchase vanished and it seemed like her captive was all body now. She kept her eyes shut and tightened her grasp to maintain her hold.

She felt hot breathe in her ear and heard a monstrous hiss. Coils of body looped around her and it was unclear whether she was holding it or it was holding her.

"A snake!" she thought. "The queen has turned him to a snake!" She kept her eyes closed and face tucked and hoped this snake would not bite her.

She felt an enormous tongue lap softly across her face.

The snake wasn't biting but it was constricting. Enormous coils pulled tighter and tighter, making it hard to breathe, and the strain of supporting the snake's entire weight was making her dizzy and likely to collapse.

"Hold on!" Morgan thought. "Don't let go."

And, after a long struggle, the chime rang a third time

She felt the snake stiffen in her arms and throw its head back violently.

And then it caught on fire.

Flames burst from its mouth and roared up and down its body. The snake threw back its head and screamed- a sound the likes of which she had never heard before.

It was quickly engulfed in flames and then Morgan began to ignite as well. She almost lost her grip then from pain and fear. "Hold on" she thought frantically "hold on!"

She screamed and heard Estelle scream as well. "Hold on Estelle!" Morgan cried "Keep holding on!"

And the troop laughed mockingly as they burned.

And the chime rang a final time.

And the flames vanished, and the signs of burning as well, and Morgan found herself holding up a naked Claud, almost fainting in her arms. Quickly she reached into her pocket, pulled out her spare rowan and red thread necklace and hung it around his neck

"Uff da indeed..." she thought, looking at the vast expanse of naked swan knight she was supporting. He leaned heavily against her, almost unconscious.

She pulled off the cloak she had intentionally worn and wrapped it quickly around him, protecting him from the cold.

Looking over, she saw that Estelle was also tending to and protecting her sister.

And now the question became how they would get away.

The queen bent down from her horse and reached out for them. Her fingers came close to Morgan and then lit up with a crackle.

"Rowan and red thread" Morgan thought. "Guess she counts enough as an evil being that it repels her."

The queen recoiled violently, and then glared at them all while blowing on her fingers.

"You have held on… so tradition and the law say that you can keep them." she said sullenly. "We shall now have to find a different teind to Hell"

Some of her troop began to look nervous.

"Now go!" the queen cried, gesturing dramatically "before I think better of my generosity!"

And the troop rode on…

…leaving them standing alone in the woods…

Chapter 41 –
Escape

The tales of adventure talk a lot about courage, and daring do, and dramatic acts.

They rarely talk about hard work, exhaustion or how frustrating some parts of those adventures could be.

Morgan and Estelle were going through the frustrating parts now.

Claud and Ariella were semiconscious and barely coherent after their time in unseelie captivity. They were bare footed and naked save only for the cloaks their rescuers had wrapped them in. They could barely hold themselves upright. Morgan and Estelle had to support them and keep them moving through the woods as best they could. The Queen and her troop had ridden on, but that didn't mean that some of them might not double back, nor that there might not be other dangers in the woods.

The cloaks weren't really doing the job either. They provided a limited amount of warmth, protection from brush and prickers, and concealment of bare flesh, but branches and breezes repeatedly pulled them out of position and they gapped with every movement the people wearing them made.

Estelle was only somewhat smaller than her sister Ariella, so it was easier for her to support her and keep her somewhat wrapped up. Morgan was slightly over five foot tall while Claud was six and a half, so her cloak mainly served as a limited gesture. The flesh exposed with every step was covered with bruises, burns and other wounds.

Captivity had not been kind to him.

He was large as well as tall and very heavy, so it was hard for Morgan to keep the semiconscious swan knight upright and moving, especially while trying not to put her hands on his injuries or in any place else they really shouldn't go.

And when he'd slump, it was hard to find leverage to bring him upright again. She knew she couldn't let him sink to the ground, because she wouldn't be able to get him back on his feet.

Sam circled from one pair to the other like a feline sheep dog, keeping watch for obstacles, urging them on and watching for pursuit.

Behind them, in the distance, they heard the blowing of horns and the sound of hooves.

Sam dashed up and said "You've got to move faster. The Queen has ridden on, but evidently some of her troop aren't willing to give up so easily. Faster, ladies!"

Estelle was ahead and began to pull Ariella along bodily. Morgan was behind them and Claud was already leaning heavily on her.

"Come on, Claud!" Morgan huffed. "I can't do this all. Show me what a swan knight can do when the chips are down."

And surprisingly, altho his face remained slack and his eyes half shut and he still leaned heavily on her, he began to pick up the pace.

They were still in trouble though. The sounds of pursuit were closer and coming up fast. There was no way they could get out of the woods before the sidhe caught up with them.

And then they heard another horn blowing far in the distance in front of them.

"Caught in the middle" thought Morgan frantically. "We're trapped. How can we possibly escape?"

And then she listened to herself and realized that once again she was setting an intention that they were going to fail.

She had another moment of clarity. What if once again she set an intention to succeed instead?

"What if this isn't an inescapable situation?" she thought. "What if this is a rescue? What if I set an intention that help is coming for us?"

She did. And she continued to think "a rescue" over and over as she hauled Claud through the woods.

And a phalanx of sidhe on horses came over the ridge in front of them, with the seelie king at the head of them.

"Ladies!" cried the seelie king genially. "I was out for a ride in this beautiful wood this evening and am pleasantly surprised to encounter you and your fellows. Might I request the pleasure of your company as we return to town?"

"Yes, please!" called out Morgan. "That would be lovely."

She heard the sound of the unseelie hunters pursuing them turn and ride away in the distance

"I guess that setting an intention stuff works..." she thought with surprise as they were helped onto horses.

Chapter 42
Wrap Up

And so it became a first aid and slumber party.

The seelie riders had wrapped the rescued prisoners in cloaks and sheepskins and various other garments until only the tips of their noses were visible, scooped them all up on horseback, offered them all food and drink, and carefully conveyed them back to Morgan and Sam's home, while glaring fiercely in the direction that pursuit had been coming from.

They gently carried Ariella and Claud up the steps and into the house, still wrapped up, and deposited them on the sofas Morgan directed them to.

"Out for a ride in the wood?" Morgan murmured to the seelie king. "Really?"

He smiled genially at her. "That is my story and I am sticking to it." he answered.

And then the seelie warriors rode away, pennants flying, their mission successfully completed.

Morgan closed the door and locked it securely before looking around the living room.

Estelle bent over her sister, gently unwrapping layers from her face and loosening the rest so she could move a bit. Ariella was still in shock, but seemed to be gradually coming back to herself.

"That's a good idea" Morgan thought, and crossed to where Claud was lying.

The seelie sidhe had wrapped him up thoroughly, and she could barely see him at all in the bundle of cloaks. She picked an end and started to unwrap what fortunately turned out to be his face.

He made a sound that might have been a whimper if he wasn't a swan knight.

"There, there" she said as she continued to ease the cloth away from his face "You're safe now, Claud. We got you away from the Queen and you're in our home."

Her fingers brushed against his face and he flinched for a moment.

"You're safe." she repeated soothingly.

His eyes opened and looked deeply into hers. He relaxed again.

"You came..." said the swan knight, with amazement in his voice. "To rescue us, you came ..."

"Well, of course" said Morgan. "Now lie still, while we get you fixed up."

She bent and began unwrapping cloaks, starting at the other end of him.

"Sam," she called out "can you bring the first aid kit and a couple of pairs of socks from the bedroom? I have some beaten up people here that need tending and warm feet."

"On it!" called the cat, from the other room. "And then can we order pizza? Hero work is hungry work."

Sam brought the kit and she began the task of tending the swan knight's wounds. His feet were torn up from stumbling through the underbrush, so she treated them with ointment and then pulled a pair of socks over them, to protect them and keep them warm, tossing the other pair of socks to Estelle for Ariella. She worked her way up his body, uncovering one section at a time and applying antiseptic, pain relief and bandages as appropriate before covering it up again.

There was a large amount of damaged swan knight flesh to tend to.

He watched her stoically.

"This is getting repetitive." she joked. "The last time you visited my home, I had to bandage you up too."

A hint of a smile tugged at the edge of his mouth. "Yah, vell, like this, ve have to stop meeting." he said. "People vil talk."

He winced as she touched one of the deeper wounds.

"Sorry about that." she said.

And then they heard the sound of a howl in the distance.

Everyone tensed. Claud sat upright, looking around wildly.

Sam was at the window in a moment, looking out. "False alarm." he said. "Just the twitchy Doberman down the street."

Morgan put a hand gently on Claud's shoulder, encouraging him to relax and lie down again, so she could continue tending his wounds.

"Don't worry." she said. "You're ok. You're in our home, and our home is warded. You're safe."

She stopped and thought.

"But safe for how long? ..." she wondered.

She froze for a moment, and then shook herself back to now.

Chapter 43
The Queen

The Queen of Air and Darkness often smiled- but she wasn't smiling now.

"Two pretty prisoners lost to me. Two pretty pretty prisoners lost."

"And two of my own subjects given for the teind instead."

"Unacceptable!" she hissed. "How did those pathetic little nothings find their way around the safeguards I had in place? How did they defeat me- the Queen of Air and Darkness?"

"This will not do." she thought. "I shall have to find a way to eliminate them as threats to my power."

She began to plan...

Glossary

Dark hund- a large unseelie fairy hound.

Dowsing- using a tool such as a pendulum, L rods or a forked stick to answer questions, find things and do other useful things.

Fairy / Fae- term for various types of fairy folk.

Glamor / glamour- illusion often used by the fae. Used to make people see what the casters wants and in extreme cases, do what the caster says.

Hearth Spirit- the protective spirit of a home.

Intention- in energy work, the goal for what you want to do with energy you are working with.

Mantelfiederfolk- the swan people.

Oubliette- a secret dungeon with access only through a trapdoor in its ceiling.

Rade / rhade- a ride or procession of trooping fairies. Dangerous to approach.

Redcap- one of the more malignant goblins. Named for his red cap which he dyes in the blood of his victims.

Seelie- those of the Sidhe considered to be more beneficent or at least benign to humans. Still can be dangerous.

Setting an intention- in energy work, choosing a target or goal for the energy you are working with.

Sidhe- a shortened form of aos sidhe, a term for the fairy People.

Teind- traditional word meaning "tithe". Usually used as part of the phrase "the teind to Hell" which was a tithe paid in captives or souls every few years.

the Lands that Lie Between- the lands of the faerie world that lie side by side with the human world like the pages of a book.

the Law of Attraction- Like attracts Like. The philosophy that the energetic level of your energy field is set by what you focus on, and the more you focus on something, the more you draw it and other things at the same vibration into your life.

Trooping sidhe- a group of the fae who use a regular practice of riding a specific path in order to gather energy.

Uff da- a general purpose expression of surprise, astonishment, exhaustion, relief and sometimes dismay. Sometimes translates to "I'm overwhelmed."

Unseelie- those of the Sidhe considered to be more actively malevolent towards humans. Definitely dangerous.

This book is dedicated to

my mother,
Janet Shoup,

Master storyteller,

Who taught me so much about caring and compassion,
Overcoming obstacles,
Achieving the impossible,
And motivating others to do the same.

We miss you, Mom.

Acknowledgements

It's visit three to The Lands that Lie Between. It takes a village to raise a child or a book, and it's important to thank that village.

Once again, many thanks to Tchipakkan, Carol and Jane, who helped me make this story a reality. Every writer should have such kind, helpful, encouraging and reliable friends and beta readers as you guys.

My gratitude to my fellow writers who encouraged me, gently nagged me, were kind and patient with me and got me writing again after a long dry spell. A writer still needs a tribe.

Love and gratitude to the people who've encouraged my writing since I was very small (and continue to do so, even though I'm still only fun sized.)

My thanks to all of the folks who've read my other books and have been politely nudging me to get more of them out into the world. This one (and all of its brothers) is for you.

And, as always, to my husband Starwolf, who is the rock that I build my writing on. Every story needs a hero, and you're still mine.

Catherine Kane was raised by feral storytellers. She's a teller of tales, a poet, a wordsmith and a songwright, an artist, an enthusiastic student of the Universe, a maker of very bad puns and a medieval re-enactor who spends a fair amount of time at renaissance faires when she isn't hunched over her computer, writing.

She's also a bit of an over-achiever.

Want to know more about her?

Find her on Facebook at
https: / / www.facebook.com / Catherine-Kane-Writes / 134304556668759

www.ingramcontent.com/pod-product-compliance
Lightning Source LLC
Chambersburg PA
CBHW061502030726
47503CB00005B/1777